OUT→

Other books by Ronald Sukenick
   Wallace Stevens: Musing the Obscure
   Up
   The Death of the Novel and Other Stories

OUT→

Ronald Sukenick

THE **SWALLOW PRESS** INC.
CHICAGO

First Edition
First Printing

Published by
The Swallow Press Incorporated
1139 South Wabash Avenue
Chicago, Illinois 60605

This book is printed on 100% recycled paper

ISBN (cloth) 0-8040-0630-X
ISBN (paper) 0-8040-0631-8
LIBRARY OF CONGRESS CATALOG CARD NUMBER 72-96165

Grateful acknowledgement is made to the following magazines in
which sections of this novel first appeared:

*Chicago Review; Fiction; Fiction International; Massachusetts
Review; Northwest Review; Partisan Review.*

$$0 \div 1 = 0$$

0

1)0‾

It all comes together. Don't fall. Each of us carries a stick of dynamite. Concealed on his person. That does several things. One it forms a bond. Two it makes you feel special. Three it's mute articulation of the conditions we live in today I mean not only us but everybody the *zeitgeist* you might say if not the human condition itself and keeps you in touch with reality. This is your stick. Don't fall. We know one among us is a government agent that's inevitable. Maybe it's you. Maybe it's me. The way we deal with that is as long as everyone does his job what's the difference. You're either part of the plot or part of the counterplot. Everybody's got to be either one or the other they all have their own opinions about which they are. Personally that's not part of my assignment. Part of it is having meets. This is a meet. The way you have meets is you take out your stick of dynamite that's your i. d. Don't fall. This is a two person meet there are bigger ones. When we get all our dynamite together we have a bomb. Then we set it off. It's all chance. Don't trust anyone you don't know that's the big thing. It's all who you like who you can work

1

with who you fuck. Personal affinity. Of course we don't have real names we have aliases. Today I'm Harrold. Two r's. Tomorrow I might be someone else. Don't fall. Of course all this probably sounds wacky to you. That's because none of it is true. It's just a joke a way we have of testing people's reactions. The dynamite stick's a dud. Light the fuse and see. Or maybe you better not. Maybe it'll blow your head off. Well you never know till you try. Right?

I'm disappointed says President Nixon. They edge across the window ledge seven floors up working their way to the left dynamite sticks in one hand the other bloodied fingertips clutching grips in stone. Beneath them long rolling lawn red brick slate shrubbery crowds of disconsolate children clump disperse circulate. Reports of fires firebombs bomb scares window smashing assaults.

I'm disappointed she repeats. Oops. She lurches sickeningly as her foot slips on the edge does an odd dance with the wall ends holding on with both hands feet firm dynamite clamped between her teeth.

Don't fall says Harrold.

I find this ridiculous mumbles President Nixon dynamite wobbling in her mouth. I come here to meet the Admiral and I find myself creeping across a window ledge with a stick of dynamite between my teeth. This isn't what I have in mind. At all. At all at all. What I want is wisdom. Enlightenment. How to live. I want to talk to the Admiral.

Harrold guffaws. I can tell you what he's going to say he mimics the old man. Plenny smokin drinkin fuckin. That's what he always says. He's just an old man.

They reach a window. Harrold winks and motions her to look inside. Inside a blond girl nude to the waist and wearing bobbysox hovers over a scrawny adolescent boy tied to a wooden chair his head hanging like a wilted flower. As they watch she grabs him by the jaws with one hand forcing his mouth open inserts a gleaming knife and severs his tongue. Blood covers his chin the severed tongue bounces off his chest and lands in his lap where it wags horribly several times in a growing pool of blood. Then she takes hold of her breast and shoves it in the boy's mouth which makes sucking motions.

President Nixon looks from the window to Harrold. Is this true she says.

9

Yo. calling all cars 7 3 10 bullseye pat em on a po po proceed with caution tough titty wrecks rex Rx i d yoo hoo hoo yoo.

This is an intercept says Scott. It's from the Commissioner.

Whose side is he on Nixie asks.

Nobody knows says Ova. What's it mean.

God knows says Rex.

It's all a lot of shid to me Jojo says. I just pass it on I do

my best.

How about asking the Comissioner says Rex.

If you can find him Scott says.

Toro says nothing.

All right says Ova. Seven plus three is ten. This is where it begins. Everybody set his watch ahead that way we have nine minutes leeway all the time. The countdown starts with nine.

Okay let's go Rex says. The alarm rings at zero.

4

Are you President Nixon asks Scott.

You're not allowed to ask that kind of question says Nixie. President Nixon is just long for Nixie.

Oh. I thought it was the other way around.

Rex and Ova go out the door together. A light is out on the landing. Rex touches Ova's arm and signals wait. Back against wall he makes his way down the stairs step by step. His hand tightens around the roll of nickels in his pocket. No one there. He waves her on. They pick their way

through the garbage on the sidewalk.

Are the meets bugged she asks.

Yes. But we don't say anything that's true. That way it doesn't matter.

We better hurry.

When does the countdown start.

I'm not sure. We still have nine minute's leeway.

Rex hails a cab. The cabbie rolls down his window.

Which way you headin he asks.

Downtown.

He rolls up his window and drives off. They pick their way through the garbage to the Avenue. Crowds of disconsolate children wander aimlessly down the side streets. Across the Avenue a cab stops for a light. Rex signals it. The cabbie rolls down the window.

Which way you headin buddy.

Uptown.

He rolls up his window and tries to lock the back door

but Rex beats him to it. They get in.
  Drive around the block says Rex. I'm in a hurry.
  Sometimes says Ova.
  Sometimes what.
  What you were wondering. In your head.
  You worry about it asks Rex.
  Sometimes. Getting hurt. Going to jail. Getting killed.
  I don't.
  No.

  No never. No point. It's all chance. Not me. Never.
Rather be surprised says Rex.
  Why worry about asks Rex.
  Hereyar says the cabbie. Rex looks for his wallet. My
wallet's lost says Rex. Ova pays. Rex opens the door. They
stroll along the garbage strewn sidewalk. Rex looks around.
His hand tightens on the roll of nickels in his pocket.
  You ready he asks.
  Ready.

  They race up the stoop into the dimlit hall up the dark
staircase bulb out at landing and stop out of breath at an
apartment door. Rex gropes through his pockets.
  The key.
  What asks Ova.
  The key the key. I can't find it.
  Oh jesus christ says Ova hurry up.
  I can't find it I can't find it.
  Hurry up I think someone's coming.

I can't find it it's lost. Yours.

I hear footsteps. What.

Yours yours use yours.

Oh my god. Here quick they're getting closer.

Open slip through slam lock the door. The footsteps pause continue up the staircase.

Who do you think that is asks Ova.

I don't know says Rex. I never worry about it. Jail. Death. Shadows. I don't think about it. What for.

Well we're here.

Yeah.

No but go ahead you have one.

Never mind I don't drink alone. It's bad luck. What's your name.

Ova. That's silly go ahead.

He shrugs and rummages through the liquor shelf. I can't find it I know it's here.

Are you a loser says Ova.

Maybe I used it up he slumps back next to her on the couch.

We better hurry she says.

Shit.

You depressed she asks.

Shit.

You are.

You ask stupid questions. Ova huh. You could think of something better than that.

It's hard after a while. Like with hurricanes.

So you know what I'm thinking.

Sometimes. You get so tuned in to everybody. A question of affinity. You've never come across it.

I can't remember.

How much time do we have.

You're always asking me that. You know I don't think about it. What for. You know I hate that.

Sorry.

Don't give me that sorry shit. You talk too much. You're full of shit.

Calm down.

Don't give me that calm down shit. I hate that. You know I hate that. I oughta bust you in the fucking teeth.

Look . . .

Don't give that look shit he screams. I oughta bust you in the fucking teeth.

He gets up and draws his fist back. She sits still hands in

lap and looks into his eyes. He hesitates then with a roar slams his fist hard against the wall. Mace hand attack.

I'll kill you he yells. Stupid cunt. You're stupid. Did you know that. And ugly. You have an ugly face. You're fat. I oughta walk right out and leave you here. You'd never get out alone you know that. They'd kill you.

I know it.

Sure you know it. You're probably working for them. What the hell you've got my mind bugged what more do they want. Was the cabbie in on it. Are you transmitting to the cabbie. Just tell me when they're going to do it that's all. Give me a hint. Knife subway accident push me off a rooftop what's it to you. You going to stick a poison suppository up my ass while I'm fucking you come on what's the story.

Fucking me.

Lemme alone.

What do you mean fucking me.

Lemme alone.

Me leave you alone hah-hah.

Fuck you look I'm sorry. You sort of fly off the handle you know you can't help it it happens to me now and then look I don't want to unload my shit on you. Tears start running out of his eyes he covers his face with his hands slumps over.

I'm not afraid of you. I don't think you're crazy. You're not a failure.

He looks up. I wish there was some whisky.

What's that stuff about fucking me Ova asks.

There's no time.

We still have nine minutes leeway.

I like you says Rex.

What do you like about me.

I like the way you're thin and have big tits.

Is that all?

No I mean I really like that kind of thing.

What kind of thing.

That kind of big tit thing. I just like it.

She sighs. Would you like to feel one.

Which one.

Either one you like. She does a shallow breast stroke and leaves her arms in the followthrough position on the back of the couch. He takes one of her breasts and holds it. She closes her eyes.

I love you says Rex.

How come.

Because you're quiet. I like quiet girls.

That's not a good reason.

You're pretty.

That's not a good reason.

I love the way you understand me. You really understand me. You can practically read my mind.

I can read your mind.

Oh yeah I forgot. I feel we're very close.

So do I.

Sometimes I feel like we're brother and sister. I felt that way before I think.

When.

I don't remember. Maybe when I was a kid. Maybe I had a sister. Sometimes I feel like we're twins. Is that a good reason.

No.

Why not.

Too familial. Would you like to hold the other one.

No thanks. One's enough right now. I love you because you're so direct.

You know why I'm so direct. Because I love you.

That's a good reason says Rcx. He kisses her.

We better hurry she says he takes her clothes off.

Yours too she says.

Why. I could fuck you with my clothes on. That could be nice.

No. The only way you can trust anybody is if thcy don't have any clothcs on. They might be carrying something.

Even my sox. What could I be carrying in my sox.

Off.

I could be carrying something anyway. I could be carrying something in my bridgework. Or up my ass. I could be carrying something in my head.

Could we just lie here first says Ova.

Okay but I can't stand it.

Oh. Oh god listen I love you. Oh jesus she says the petals part the flower opens blind blunt bumble bump blunder blunder he barges in her flesh turns to honey sticky glistening throbbing he slides to a stop.

This is the start of a journey he says. I don't know how long it will be or where it takes you no one ever does. All you can do is keep track. You keep track with your head. Your head tells you where your body goes. The important thing is never stop talking. If you forget the words make sounds make new words. Make words that grunt scream laugh hum sob. The voice is the connection between the body and the head. Silence means you're lost. Or that you're there. Or both. Or both. Or both. Uh. Or both. Uh.

Are you the Commissioner she asks.

I have. Uh. Commission. Oo. Address. Ah.

Wait she says. Please. I love you. Wait for me.

Ooo he says. Oh. Ah. Ah.

Please. Wait.

He sounds a sudden short gutteral like a man kicked in the belly. She a scream.

You hurt me she says.

Sorry.

It was like a gunshot.

Sorry.

You were just checking. To see if I'm carrying something there. Well there's nothing there are you happy. Do you want to check my anus.

Are you an agent. They got a friend of mine that way. First degree sodomy. They used a seventeen year old girl. Bugged her asshole. As soon as he stuck it in it set off an alarm. Town upstate.

You're just checking me out admit it.

I love you. Even if you are an agent. I thought you could read my mind.

Not any more I can't. Not any more. Get dressed. We better hurry.

Don't worry I have his address.
Who is he.
All I have is his address. What's the hurry says Rex.
I said I'm sorry says Rex.
Can't you believe that says Rex.
I love you says Rex.
I really do says Rex.
What can I say says Rex.
Answer me you know what happens if you stop talking

says Rex.
You strangle. That's why they cut your tongue out. It's better than castration says Rex.
Ready says Rex.
He turns on the radio all the lights latches the windows locks the window grates sets up the bar for the police lock out the door lock the police lock lock the regular lock Ova breathes in. This is a stickup says a guy knife point pricking her larynx don't move or she gets hurt.

Okay okay says Rex. Take it easy don't get nervous.
I'm not nervous I'm not nervous. Shud up. Gimme your money.
Ova digs in her bag hands him her wallet. He looks through it takes out the bills. That it he asks.
Yes. I want my wallet back says Ova.
Sure says the guy here thanks.
You're welcome says Ova.
What about you says the guy.

I don't have any cash says Rex. Will you take a check.
I don't know says the guy. You got any i. d.
Yeah I guess so.
Ah the hell with it. Well have a nice evening he says
backing away knife arm extended. And don't move till I
get downstairs. Sorry for bothering you.
Not at all says Rex. Come back again.
Ova rubs a tiny red mark on her throat. You all right
says Rex. Could've been a lot worse.

We better hurry says Ova. She holds his arm as they go
down the stairs. He feels her hand shaking. His fist tightens
around the roll of nickels in his pocket. On the ground
floor a man lounges in the vestibule between the inner and
outer doors.
Let's go out through the courtyard says Rex. I don't like
the looks of that guy. They go down the back stairs through
the courtyard past the garbage cans in the dimdamp tunnel
alongside the basement toward the sidewalk Ova breathes

in. This is a stickup says a guy knife point at her throat
don't move or she gets hurt.
Look you just hit us says Rex.
Oh shid sorry. You can't see a fuckin thing down here.
Shid you oughta stay outa these dark courtyards they're
dangerous.
Yeah thanks for the tip. They come up the stairs to the
sidewalk.
My name's Jose says the guy.

Hi says Rex. I'm Carl. This is Velma.

I'm a junkie says Jose.

I thought so says Carl.

Everybody calls me Jojo you know why because I'm always clowning around. Like the other day this guy says to me what are you wise an I let em have it right in the face. Right in his fuckin face says Jojo. Was he surprise man.

Yeah I got a habit says Jojo. That's why I rob you before.

That's what I thought says Carl.

We better hurry says Velma.

They start walking down the street. Jojo gives Velma a proprietary pat on the ass hey man watch the dogshid he says. Velma sidesteps a fresh dog turd.

Shid that musta been a St. Bernard shooting Ex Lax. You gotta watch it with them shoes you got. She your girlfriend asks Jojo.

We better hurry says Velma. They walk faster zigzagging through the garbage faster dodging dogturds faster past the

glass storefronts the tenement entrances now they're almost running Jojo effortless keeps pace neck pumping like a galloping giraffe as if it drives his whole body. Something about the alignment of his neck and back terrifies Carl. The way they form an absolutely straight line.

I'm a junkie says Jojo that's why I steal.

That's what I thought says Carl. Faster.

Shid it's harder than you think man. I mean the risks I gotta take man. I mean all I get outa you is thirteen lousy bucks man. Like how do I know what you carryin you could be carryin a gun man. Like I could get kill man. Like that's a lot a shid man. The faster Carl walks the faster Jojo talks. Jojo takes some bills out.

Look why don't you take some a this back lady. Shid I don't need your money man. Shid thirteen's my unlucky number man. Shid I don't need your shid man. Like they steal your body and then you gotta pay them rent that's what it is man. I gotta pay them rent on my body. Shid

thiroof. Carl catches him with a right roundhouse kick to the gut a left knife hand to the bridge of the nose as he doubles over and finishes him with an upper target punch to the larynx fist gripped on roll of nickels.

Keep walking says Carl Jojo still falling. They turn down a side street lined with fire escapes. Men squat on the sidewalks the stoops look like the bleachers at the Yankee-Dodger Series 1947. Kids drift back and forth across the street in shifting crowds.

The address says Velma.

The what.

The Commissioner's address. We better hurry.

Carl takes a little leather bound red book out of his pocket and looks through it carefully.

I've lost it he says.

What do we do now.

The zoo.

What zoo.

I have a meet at the zoo. Just in case. The tiger cage.
Who with.
I forget.
Everything starts moving twice as fast. The squatting
men get up change places squat down twice as fast. The
women on the stoops talk twice as fast. Baby carriages careen
down the sidewalks twice as fast. The kids drift across the
street and back twice as fast and there are twice as many of
them. The cars coming down the street come twice as fast

behind them come three police cruisers sirens blasting.
Everything starts moving three times as fast. There are
three times as many as everything and it's all whizzing along
the sidewalks the curbs the gutters the middle of the street
and it's going both ways. People bump into one another a
baby carriage overturns there's a collision down at the
corner between a pushcart and a bus. A kid runs into
Velma and almost knocks her over. Everybody's running
one way down the middle of the street toward something

away from something Carl can't tell. Faster he says.
I can't says Velma. Please. Wait for me. Carl catches up
to a man running with a transistor radio at his ear. What's
going on Carl asks.
There's been another escalation says the man.
Another one.
There's gonna be a demonstration you wanna go.
Another one.
This one's gonna be different.

Why.

I don't know.

Galloping trotting finally walking the people emptying from the street lose themselves in the flux of a crowd filling an open square. Waves of words from the P. A. system wash back and forth through the air. We we we free free free we we we dom dom dom dom free free free now now now dom dom dom dom want want we we we we.

Where's Velma says the transistor guy.

Velma Carl says.

Velma Carl yells.

Carl cups his hands around his mouth. Velma he yells. Velma. Velma.

A wedge of shiny blue helmets appears at one side of the square goggles rubber trunks moves slowly out into the crowd which parts recedes moves back toward the helmets with the surge of people from behind. A rock flies through the air a bottle smashes.

We better get out of here says Carl.

Who's Velma.

I don't know. Why. Have you seen her says Carl.

Everyone is yelling. It sounds like someone's just hit a homer. Nightsticks flash up and down. One or two bottles smash. Several bricks fly into the air. Stones tin cans garbage. Two black teenagers holding up signs advance toward the wedge the lid of a trash can sails toward the helmets. An explosion resonates through the square another. Five or six more. The man running in front of Carl stumbles over a girl lying on the pavement falls as Carl swivels sidesteps the pileup bulling full speed past anyone in his way. Gas rises in slow creamy clouds jagged cumuli tumuli spreading along the ground. Carl rips around the corner sprints down the street slows to a walk. He has a sore throat. Sirens are coming from everywhere. At the next corner he stops to buy a paper. The headline says CROWD GASSED IN SQUARE FLEES. He sits down in a cross-

town bus and opens his paper. Behind him another man gets on sits opens his paper. The headline says GASSED CROWD RETURNS TO SQUARE. Carl leaves his paper on the seat and gets off to wait for an uptown. The man gets off waits at the same busstop. Now he's reading Carl's paper. Carl gets on the bus the man gets on the bus. Carl sits down the man sits down right behind him. Carl feels he's being followed he absorbs himself in the sights out the window buildings cars people walking on the sidewalk. At

the zoo the man gets off. Carl also gets off at the zoo. The man walks into the park Carl walks into the park. The man seems to be following the zoo signs. Now Carl follows the man. Yet when Carl arrives at the zoo the man isn't there. How do you explain that. Coincidence?

The tiger. The tiger is upset. She runs back and forth in her cage switching her tail and making faces with her teeth the lines on her muzzle fine as ticking whiskers a white holocaust. If she roars the world ends. Carl is at a fence two feet away from the bars of the cage. He wants to leave. If he doesn't leave something terrible is going to happen to him but his body won't move. His body likes that other bigger body behind the bars likes its bigness likes its gravity it's a more serious body than his own it draws him he wants to merge with it embrace it be consumed destroyed he doesn't he begins to shake and sweat. A man steps over the fence old khaki shirt old khaki pants a face like a thousand other faces. Don't says Carl.

It's a little oily says the man.

For what says Carl. The man speaks in an old time Brooklyn accent Carl recognizes it. You don't hear them much any more.

She don't get this way so oily says the man. Sometin's eatiner. What's eatin yiz Princess. Comere hey.

Don't says Carl.

Yuh gotta talk to em dey like dat. I don care what animal you gotta make friends widem. Yuh gotta talk to em den yuh gotta touch em. Come on hey what's wrong witchez Princess. Come on hey. Come on pussy. Comere hey. Atta goil atta goil.

The tiger pads back and forth closer and closer to the bars. The man in khaki sticks his arm into the cage through the bars to the shoulder.

Don't says Carl.

The tiger heads teeth bared toward the outthrust arm then veers toward the other end of the cage. Her fangs are thick as the man's wrist.

Comere baby comere pussy what's wrong witchez atta goil atta goil dats right dats right.

I'll scream says Carl.

The tiger pads snarling toward the motionless hand then veers so it just touches her shoulder. She turns passes again this time letting it run along her neck down her side. The man draws his hand back to the bars and the tiger passes along the bars allowing the hand to run down the length of

her body. Again and again she rubs along the bars the man's hand caresses her body his fingers leave long furrows in the fur.

Dere just like housecats. Bigger dat's all.

Now he's petting her nape her spine her passes are slower. She rubs her ear along the bars he presses his head against her head kisses her on the cheek just behind the open mouth. Carl feels faint.

Dat's all Princess now go lie down. She does two turns

around the cage then pads into a corner lies down. She follows him with her head as he climbs back over the fence.

How do you do that asks Carl.

Keep talkin says the man in khaki. Make friends witcha tongue.

How do you mean.

I gotta go says the man.

Wait.

When ya gotta go ya gotta go. He goes.

Just then the tiger roars. The world ends. Then it begins again. When Carl looks the man in khaki is gone another man is there instead.

You forgot your paper says the man.

What paper.

On the bus. Here.

Oh thanks says Carl. This man is blond and wears a business suit. Carl is dark collar open leather vest.

My name is Carl says the blond man. What's yours.

Donald says Carl.

Hi there Donald. Carl extends his hand and Donald shakes it. Hello Carl says Donald.

Say look at this says Carl. He snaps open his attache case Donald has time to see a note taped to the inside cover before he snaps it closed. The note says I'm looking for the Commissioner.

Well I gotta go says Carl.

Hey wait.

Carl is already three steps away moving fast. Hey wait says Donald.

I gotta go says Carl. Donald doesn't catch up with him until Carl enters the men's room.

When you gotta go you gotta go says Carl heading for the urinal. Hey look at this. He unzips his fly pulls out a thick red tube with a string at the end.

That's dynamite says Donald.

Yeah got a light.

Is it real.

Light it and see says Carl.

I have one too says Donald.

You're Jewish aren't you.

Why.

You're swarthy and smart. Why don't you come home with me I'd like you to meet my wife.

They go outside for a cab. At the corner of the avenue Carl raises his index finger gazes sternly into space exposes

his cuspids and gives a shrill whistle. Two cabs practically collide as they scream to a stop Carl ushers Donald into one of them while the cabbies argue about whose fare they are. Donald thinks about the cabs on the way to Carl's. Why can't he whistle between his teeth that way broods Donald. Is it because he's Jewish is he really swarthy and smart. Or is he dark and brooding the way he likes to think of himself. They get out upstairs a blond girl in a tennis outfit answers the door. This is Ova says Carl.

You're not Ova says Donald Ova has auburn hair and I think freckles.

I'm a different Ova she says. Do you believe in the myth of vaginal orgasm.

I haven't thought about it.

You and I are going to have a discussion says Ova. Let me put on something more appropriate.

Wait a minute says Carl. Make the soup.

Now. Oh gee. Why now.

24

We have to give Donald his soup that's what he's here for right.

If you say so says Donald. What kind of soup.

What kind of soup. Very cool. You're very cool do you know that Donald. Open the can what are we calling you Ova. They go into the kitchenette and watch Ova as she opens a can of alphabet soup empties it into a sauce pan warms it on the stove takes down three bowls.

Now says Carl. She divides the soup among the three

bowls. Carl picks a letter out of his bowl with a spoon places it on his napkin. Then another then another then another picking placing rearranging. When he has a line of letters arranged to his satisfaction he shows it to them. It says abcdefghijklmnopqrstuvwxyz.

O wow says Ova. She does the same thing with her soup. So does Donald.

Now says Carl. He takes out a pair of dice shakes them rolls. A seven and a three.

Now says Carl. Seven and three is ten. He nods to Ova. Pick the first seven letters out of your bowl. Ova picks t h e c o m m.

Now I pick the next three from mine. Carl picks i s s.

Now Donald ten. Donald picks i o n e r d i i n g.

That's fantastic says Donald.

What's it mean says Ova.

Dying says Carl. It's misspelled.

By who asks Ova.

He's dying says Carl.

I can't believe it says Donald. Before I talk to him.

Easy says Carl.

But he can't just leave us like that. Forever.

Don't grieve says Carl. Organize. That's the way he would want it.

God god god. Donald slumps over the table.

Besides says Ova putting her hand on Donald's shoulder maybe there's still time.

That's right. What letters are left in your bowl says Carl.

I have an i says Donald.

I have an o says Carl.

I have nothing says Ova what does that mean.

Nothing means nothing.

What does i mean.

It means you win. I trumps o. I is more than o. I is one o is zero. One destroys nothing and recreates it. It means i o you.

Owe me what.

Ten. One and zero is ten. Ten is Io the cow. Ova is Io. I is sterile o is empty. One into zero is nothing.

Ova gets up. I have to put on something more appropriate she says she goes out.

What's her real name.

Nadia says Carl. O needs i i needs o. I o is yo. This is a message from the Commissioner. Yo is his code signature. Now we have to eat the message.

To destroy it?

To understand it. Words come out of the body into the air. Then they have to come out of the air back into the body. He puts the letters back into the three bowls. Nadia comes in wearing a micromini and a transparent blouse. Carl and Donald stare at her her lips open in surprise her blue eyes are empty o's of innocence her straight blond hair frames her oval face they eat their soup.

I have something to confess to you says Carl he takes out

a bottle of whisky. Drink. No thanks says Donald Carl pours himself a drink. Donald feels Nadia's thigh against his knee under the table.

I have something to confess to you Carl isn't my real name. That's because I'm not real. I'm only trying to be real. Like a character in a novel. He pours himself a drink. But you're real that's why I like you. Nadia's thigh starts moving up and down against Donald's knee. You're real but you have no personality. It's all personality that's why

you're a flop. You change all the time nobody knows where you're at not even you. I may be a character but at least I'm not a flop. He pours a drink Donald can feel the meat of Nadia's thigh flopping against his knee.

Nadia isn't a flop either says Carl. She's not even a character she's an empty hole.

Oh Carl says Nadia.

She may not be a flop but she likes to flop he he he I'm getting drunk. That's because she's a cow. Cowflop is good luck. If she doesn't flop she flips. Flip flop. I'm just a character trying to be a person the strain is terrific. I think I'll leave you two alone now good luck he staggers into another room.

So you're part of the gang says Nadia.

What gang.

The bang gang. That's what I like to call it. Because of the dynamite where's yours. In your pants. She reaches over and feels his pants. Here it is. She giggles. I've found it.

Give it to me.

That's not it says Donald.

It is. She gets down on her knees. If you don't give it to me I'm going to bite it she bites it not too hard harder.

Watch it it's going to explode. She gets up turns around look under my skirt she says. He lifts her skirt finds two bare cheeks smooth round. That's my i.d. she says. Study it carefully so you'll recognize it again. My code name is the White Ass. Carl's the same thing but with a p for an s. P

for penis. I showed you mine you show me yours. She unzips his fly sits down on

8

it it's going to explode. The alarm rings he wakes up turns it off picks up the phone dials YO 7-7310.

Hello.

Hello is this information.

For what phase.

Eight.

Eight you're it they hang up Harrold replaces the receiver.

He sticks his finger into a hump on the other side of the bed. Pack up. We're moving he says.

She opens her eyes blinks. Again. Why.

Why because we're moving. Why.

Who was that on the phone says Trixie.

That was the Governor. I'm it. Come on start packing.

We just moved says Trixie. And we just moved before that. And before that and before that.

28

Get dressed says Harrold. Start packing. I'm it.

You never fuck me any more says Trixie.

I never fuck you says Harrold. I never fuck you you never want to.

I never want to you never ask me.

You never look like you want me to ask you.

I don't look like I want you to ask me because you don't want to ask me.

I don't think I should have to ask you. Why should I have to kiss your ass. For a piece of ass?

So I'm just a piece of ass is that it.

Yeah you're just a piece of ass. Fuck you.

Fuck you. Find somebody else.

That's exactly what I intend to do.

You find somebody else I'll cut your prick off.

I'll beat your ass so black and blue nobody'll look at it.

You'll have to beg for cock in the streets.

You'd like that.

I can't stand this I'm splitting.

Good go ahead says Trixie.

First we have to move. Get dressed.

What do we do with all our stuff.

Put it in the cartons.

It doesn't fit in the cartons.

Leave it here.

Not my stuff says Trixie.

Throw it in the U-Haul says Harrold.

Cover me while I go downstairs says Trixie. He opens the door steps into the hall flattens himself against the wall the bulb is out on the landing go on he says I'm watching. She runs for it down the stairs past the plasterpeeled walls around large cracks in the floor past the sign that says this

hall is a bomb shelter to the super's apartment she knocks at the door.

Who.

Trixie quick.

The door opens a crack then wider. I can't let anybody in here you know that shid they take everything you got says Jojo.

Jojo can you help take our things down to the U-Haul.

Whatsa matter you movin.

No we're just taking our things down to the U-Haul.

Shid man you smart man they take everything you got man. You know that man up in 4A they even take his bed they clean him out. An he's a junkie too man you know what him and his friends done man they steal all the copper pipes in the place next store then they go down and take all the brass fittings off the furnace so they ain't got no heat or hot water in the whole building man somebody oughta call the cops on that guy.

Did you.

Nah he's a friend a mine come on in for a beer.

I can't Harrold is upstairs we've got to get the things down.

I say come on in for a beer split a joint you got time what the hell. He your boyfriend.

I can't he's waiting we have to move the things.

Okay look what I'll do I watch the U-Haul you don't have to worry about it okay.

Trixie and Harrold start moving the stuff down. When Trixie goes down the stairs Harrold covers her when Harrold goes down the stairs Trixie covers him Jojo takes the stuff from the stoop to the U-Haul they work hard and steady then Harrold comes down to lock the U-Haul.

Hey somebody rob your U-Haul says Jojo.

What do you mean.

There's nothin in there man them guys are smart I don know how they done it I was watchin alla time.

Where's Trixie I thought she was down here.

She your girlfriend man she's a terrific piece of ass.

Where is she is she in your place.

She ain't in my place come on back an take a look they

go back to Jojo's apartment.

See what I mean I tell you man.

Where is she.

Don ask me she aint my girlfriend. I bet she's a terrific lay.

Don't get smart let's check the street they go back outside the U-Haul is gone. So is the car hauling it. What the fuck says Harrold.

Maybe the girl took it says Jojo she can't drive says Harrold.

Maybe she found a driver what a you care man them U-Haul people got insurance.

How am I going to move says Harrold.

Where you movin to.

Brooklyn.

So it's simple you catch the BMT at Union Square now

you got nothin to carry you're all set.

Harrold drifts down the sidewalk through the garbage the dogturds to the corner. A bus stops Harrold gets on drops the fare sits down starts crying. Tears roll down his cheeks sobs tear up from his belly his trunk jerks back and forth his head bobs up and down he sounds like he's going to sneeze. The man next to him gets up moves to another seat. Hic hic hic says Harold hic hic hic he can't stop nearby passengers get up change their seats muh muh muh says Harrold his nose drips his face red and twisted his voice waivers m-u-u-h m-u-u-h m-u-u-u-u-h. M-U-U-H he howls M-U-U-H M-U-U-U-U-H. Passengers ring for a stop the bus stops only at bus stops says the driver AAAAAA screams Harrold AAAAAAAAAAAA AA AAAA AAAA-AAAAAAAA the driver stops the bus I think we got a nut here he says into his radio. A fat old lady gets up waddles

down the aisle sits next to Harrold. She rummages through her shopping bag takes out a kleenex here she says wipe your nose.

Hic hic hic says Harold.

Yes that's right says the old lady here wipe your nose.

Hic hic hic I don't want to gasps Harrold the old lady grabs his nose with the kleenex blow she says he takes the kleenex wipes his nose. Let's see your hand says the old

lady she looks like a fat peanut no your palm she says she holds his hand in her smaller chubbier hand. Psychic or visionary she says.

What.

That's the pointed type avoid schedules but watch out for indigestion let's see. You have a well-developed middle finger good heart line you like the opposite sex look at that mount of venus. Avoid premature ejaculation. You have a roving restless disposition and have suffered many disappointments *beware of head wounds* and encourage mental developments wait a minute. Let's get a closer look at that line of destiny. Oh. She closes his hand and gives it back to him. You have a prominent plain of mars that's hope. Put your faith in that you're going to need it.

But what about the line of destiny.

I have to get off here she rings the buzzer.

But what about the line of destiny.

I have to go now here's my card she gives him a card. Cultivate the unexpected it's your only chance she gets up.

But wait.

I have to go now.

Wait.

Hope for surprises welcome the unknown. Remember.

But the line of destiny.

When you have to go you have to go. She goes Harrold looks at her card. It says this was no accident Ali Buba fortune teller. He gets off at Union Square there's a locked grate across the subway entrance he walks down the street wave of horn blaring comes from somewhere up ahead sweeps along triple line of stalled traffic peaks spends itself behind in ragged diminuendo junkies rock back and forth near buildings twisted in impossible postures winos dribble

into gutter seedy old men walk in and out of automat
muttering one ancient specimen shuffles along trunk bent
at ninety degree angle from waist beard grazing sidewalk
old lady picks through trash can from around corner a
woman screams once twice long drawn out third two cops
in patrol car laugh with fat man leaning through their
window clumps of black schoolchildren in chartreuse pants
immense flat yellow peaked caps wander along street break

into aimless gallops merge turn go back the other way fire
engines howl up side street sound of breaking glass Harrold
has the feeling something unusual is going to happen he
steps into a nearby high school to get out of its way whatever it is a tall thin black comes toward him waving a stick
Harrold runs up crosshatched metal steps walled by glass
covered chickenwire red metal bannisters ceiling bulbs in
wire cages comes out into long corridor three of them

behind necks pumping like galloping giraffes not so much
after Harrold as away from something else the alarm rings
he finds another stair runs down out on the street finds an
open entrance takes the Sea Beach Express changes to the
Graves End Local gets off at Avenue I come down the
metal steps of the El a dog lifts its head off the sidewalk
starts wagging its tail. A large mutt with spots and hanging
ears sounds a high pitched whine ending in a deep bark

starts to get up slips wags tail whines blats a rubbery fart
makes it up onto its front legs shoves its grey pink moth-
eaten muzzle into the air snuffs wags harder slowly
straightens up its back legs barks stretches wags farts limps
over presses its muzzle against my knee groans sighs it smells
awful I pat its head. The dog shakes its ears sneezes limps
off a few feet looks back barks wags walks arthritically
down Avenue I I follow past hedges and concrete stoops

after a block we turn left down East 2nd Street and the
smell of burning leaves stings my eyes past thick black-
brown timbers of scary coalyard gloomy sheds invisible
horse exhalations clop clop vague bronx cheers across dirt
road through hedge down grasy bank to curving railroad
grade of trunk line up high wide grassy shoulder looking
steeply down to main cut steam engine bursts out tunnel
down cut hooting puffing still have cowcatchers boxcars

flatcars boxcars flatcars boxcars boxcars boxcars man in
caboose waving pigeon lands on hightension wire blam-
poof explodes like cherry bomb out under El down Graves
End over railroad yard along trolley tracks. The dog whines
rubs its shoulder against my leg looks up at me what's
wrong old sport what can I do for you. It barks runs lum-
bering along Gravesend barking out of deep caverns of its
dogness looking back going around in little circles.

Terhune heel!

It lumbers back rubs its shoulder against my legs whines looks up at me I notice a note attached to its collar. I pull it off it says meet me in the lot Arthur is it Artie is this a meet my mind goes reeling down Gravesend under the calm rumble of the El from way down the track so low you can hardly hear it at first the slow rumble of the El so loud you can hardly hear anything else down Gravesend toward the

vacant lot the calm rumble of the El I can hear even after I stop hearing it way way down the track.

I follow Terhune to the lot behind hedges fencing grape arbors chickens pigeons rabbits of the backyards of the neighborhood Terhune limps tailwagging through the brown belthigh weeds through the deeper bushes rusting cans shattered bottles broken bricks to the hideout. Where in a bare spot in the highest weeds the thickest thickets

Artie stares unconsoled at the charred leavings of an old campfire. Hi Artie.

Don't call me Artie says Artie. You know that.

It's your name isn't it.

My name is Arthur.

Then how come we always call you Artie.

That's my nickname. My real name is Arthur. I was named after an English king.

Which one.

Arthur.

How come.

Because we came down from English kings. On my father's side.

Really. How do you know.

My father told me.

I don't believe it.

Artie gets up. Are you going to call my father a liar. My father's a mailman. He gives me a light push.

Okay Arthur. I didn't know your father was a mailman.

Damn right he is says Artie. He sits down and stares at the cold charwood he does look a lot like royal blood straight nose straight upper lip straight eyebrows pale golden hair long pale face maybe there's a royal bastard in his background I don't bring that up not with his father

a mailman. But how come you're Arthur today when you're Artie the rest of the time.

Because I ran away today.

Again how come.

Because I hate my father.

How come.

He's a bastard. I hate him.

Gee Artie. Do you want me to bring you something to

eat.

I'll make out there's a message for you.

Where.

Under the rock.

I stick my hand under the rock and pull out a piece of crumpled yellow paper. The writing on it looks like it was done by a small child or someone in a tremendous hurry or someone with his hands tied behind his back holding

the pencil in his teeth. It says celebrate inhaled student cards. Includes cabbie's birthday. Or maybe celibate male stud in trouble. Elude scabs Thursday. Or maybe calibrate mail studies up tight. Need crabs thirsty.

Who's it from I ask.

Ontday onay says Artie.

What.

Ontday Onay. Oundfay erethay.

Did you find it.

Ixnay.

I fold the note up and put it in my pocket Artie gets up. Come on he says.

Where.

They're getting up a stickball game.

We head over to Kent's. Kent is a serious person. He always knows what we're going to do and how we're going to do it. We always try to find out from Kent what to do. The left side of my face starts twitching and my left eye narrows to a slit a lot like Downwind in Smilin' Jack also I start to limp. That's what Kent does and it really feels right. We cut through a fence and limp into Kent's yard Kent limps over carrying his roller skates you getting up a stickball game says Artie.

Who says says Kent we're going skating his face twiches.

I don't have my skates I say.

You can watch says Kent we limp out toward East Second. Why skating Kent says Artie Kent frowns. His face twitches twice as fast. His left eye goes on and off like a blinker light.

Why skating says Kent. Why skating. Skating is a very ancient sport. The first known instances of skating are recorded in Egyptian hieroglyphs chiseled into the pha-

roahs' tombs. They appear shortly after the invention of the wheel some say before. However the sport seems to have disappeared with the destruction of antiquity along with so much else. Some Mohammedan scholars claim that it was preserved in the Sufic tradition and certainly it has much in common with the *but en soi* orientation of some Sufic Masters as witness Jalaludin Rumi's paradigm of which Rilke was so fond about the identity of wick with flame. Let us not though overstate the case I merely wish to make the distinction between a traditional and self-contained activity like skating which requires no justification and a game like stickball invented by ignorant children in city streets and in any case derivative of more adequate versions of ball and bat sports.

As he walks his limp and his twitch start to join up so that the left side of his body resembles an ongoing spastic con-

vulsion. I just screw up the left half of my face and leave it there I can't keep up with that. Kent is a little older. Maybe in a few years we'll be able to do it as well as him though I doubt it.

Between the burning of the library at Alexandria by Heliogabulus and the Renaissance we draw a blank though there are certain hints in Dante and then suddenly we find a mechanical sketch of the skate reinvented or was it

merely rediscovered in Leonardo's notebooks. I am not attempting to recreate history you understand but to examine a tradition and its meaning. Is it mere coincidence that skating reenters history at the peak of the Renaissance I like to think not. Skating is too much the embodiment of that Renaissance ideal of cultivated balance known as *sprezzatura* for us to be dealing with mere historical accident. Nor can we completely discount the possibility that

Leonardo was himself in touch with that secret international cult of wisdom of poets statesmen beggars of Christian Jew Mohammedan of natural nobility whose impact on our civilization is so incalculable. The similarities between the Italian ideal and the Sufic one speak for themselves and we may even speculate that Leonardo was himself a secret Master. Certainly some such tradition may have existed then may in fact still exist I do not speak of

such derivative parodies as the Freemasons. Certainly such men may still exist must exist Dixie Walker for instance. What better summary of the teaching indeed than Lawrence's motto I mean D. H. glad sure and indifferent. Maybe we are all gifted with a secret wisdom we are unable to utter. Maybe we need to speak with tongues.

What does that mean Kent.

I don't know says Kent. Kent sits down on the curb he

looks depressed.

I thought we were going to go skating says Artie I can't says Kent.

Why not.

I forgot my skate key.

You want me to get it for you says Artie.

Let's you and me go together Kent pulls himself up.

What about him says Artie.

He's Jewish they limp off together.
Are you leaving me flat I say.
Are you leaving me flat I yell.
Artie looks over his shoulder yeah he says.
Flat leavers I yell.
Larry Lloyd and Lance come down the street walking three abreast because they're brothers. Hi Larry I say. Hi Lloyd. Hi Lance.

Roosevelt or Wilkie says Larry.
Roosevelt Larry belts me in the face.
I get up holding my lip. Hey.
Roosevelt or Wilkie says Lloyd.
Roosevelt Lloyd belts me in the stomach. I get up shaking my head hey come on.
Lance is smaller than me. Roosevelt or Wilkie he says.
Wilkie Larry and Lloyd grab my arms and Lance kicks

me in the balls I start crying.
Crybaby they say they let me go and walk on down the street. I go over to the cut Big Bish is there. So are Dominick Salvador and Vince so is dumb Gerard so is Murphy the ball player so is Gino who was kicked out of school so is Zip the nitwit so is Mickey the Armenian tough Tony blond Tim who wears baby blue Herbie the klutz Teddy the Greek Nick the Greek Nick the Wop O'Toole the fire-

man's son Alvin the Polack who I beat up they're putting out a grass fire. O'Toole tells everybody what to do everybody does as he pleases Bish is pushing Tim around for exercise and fun Gerard is cursing Tim is telling Bish to cut it out Herbie and Nick are working hard Nick is goofing off Zip lights matches and stares at them with his buggy eyes and most everybody else is standing around.

Come on says O'Toole head it off before it hits the

tracks.

Who says says Tony.

I say.

Who are you.

It's my fire I started it says O'Toole.

Something tells me to look down I bend over pick a two dollar bill off the ground a brick floats through the air where my head was hurtles into the grass Gerard five

feet behind me face red still in his followthrough.

Why'd you do that I say Gerard shrugs I hit Gerard about fifteen times in five seconds without knowing it mostly in the stomach. Gerard is lying on the ground he's bigger than me but he doesn't get up I open my fist I'm still holding the two dollar bill.

You're lucky says Bish. If I were you I'd check out the Pontiff he loves lucky people take Lucky Luciano. Or

Louis Lepke Buchalter he's Jewish you know. Those guys live in the neighborhood they talk about them in the barber shop but not too much. Or too loud. I'd go over there if I were you get a haircut who knows.

I walk up out of the cut to the corner pull the fire alarm and get the hell out of there. By a shortcut through an alley behind the coalyard horse cloppings exhalations why are we afraid to go in there. I bet Joe the barber knows

about it. He's old white hair skin the color of an old tobacco pipe he speaks Italian most of the time. I bet he knows a lot only I don't know what to ask him. He has a very big head the only person who has a bigger one is my dad and his is bigger than anyone's. I walk into the barber shop.

Watch you want sonny.

Can I have a glass of water.

Shoe says Joe. You get. Then you go home. I betch they lookin for you.

On East Second you can smell the burning leaves. It's getting cold. The vegetable man keeps pulling his sweater down over his wrists as he pushes his cart. Nanaw he yells. Nanaw. Nanaw. He looks like bananas himself his nose is a banana. He walks like he's made of bananas. I cross East Second to 101 I on the corner. Terhune is waiting by the

door he starts to wag his tail I go in.
  Who's there.
  I'm looking for the Commander-in-Chief.
  Who wants him.
  The Crown Prince.
  What for.
  I have to ask him something.
  What.

  I don't know.
  He's busy you can't bring that dog in here he's just a puppy.
  I found him he followed me.
  He belongs to somebody else he's not housebroken. You're allergic to dogs.
  I'm not.
  Did you pull that fire alarm. Wait till your father comes

in. You're going right to bed you're sick you have a fever. I told you not to go out were you in the cut again were you playing with those kids. What do you want to ask your father why don't you ask me.

  I can't. I look out the door for Terhune but he's run away I can just see him way down the other end of East Second I start crying.

  What is it now I don't know what I'm going to do with

you you're sick you're going to bed. In bed I can hear the
ladies in their high heels going by tic toc tic toc tic toc way
down the street. I can hear the coalman's wagon passing the
clop clop of his horse the flutter of its exhalations. The slow
clack and rumble of the El starts way off toward Coney
Island. It's a long time ago.

Somebody's beating on the door with a gun butt he lies
still what

7

time is it. The thudding continues he doesn't breathe. Then it stops. He looks at his watch it's seven A. M. He waits fifteen minutes gets out of bed puts on his pants looks through the peephole opens the door a crack a telegram falls to the floor. He slams the door tears open the envelope it says get rid of the cat. And get out of town regards President Roosevelt. The cat the neighborhood is

full of cats all hungry most diseased torn and twisted. This one comes mewing pathetically through the window from the fire escape a kitten unbelievably thin walking sort of sideways to focus with its one good eye the other is swollen four times as big and looks like a round piece of charcoal with the outline of a pupil on its black crust. Every now and then the thing paws its eye falls down and writhes

48

around for a while. He gives it a plate of milk then he goes and vomits. The next day it comes back in then it comes twice a day three times then he starts counting the number of times it goes out he wonders when it's going to die soon he hopes. It keeps getting thinner if that's possible the eye bulges farther and farther out of its head. He can't look at the thing without wanting to vomit. Sometimes he feels

like vomiting then he looks at it. He vaguely hopes something will happen to it next time the apartment is robbed a junkie might stab it or steal it for ransom or some fucking thing. The apartment is robbed about once a month which isn't bad for the neighborhood. He still has a bed refrigerator and kitchen table when they run through those items he can just leave. He's tired of the place and

he's tired of the cat. He's tired of vomiting. Now the cat is beginning to vomit he's tired of that too. President Roosevelt is right. Get rid of the cat. And leave town why doesn't he think of these things himself.

He gets a heavy shopping bag and lays it on its side the kitten is having one of its seizures a thin fluid from its mouth puddles on the floor he pushes the thing into the bag with his foot ties the top closed with a cord. He can feel it bumping around scratching feebly against the bag. Unlock the door look through peephole light out on landing go out slam door lock police lock regular lock edge to stairs dash down two at a time through corridor into street he hears a long thin yowl again again he bangs the bag against the building it starts trying to claw its way out of

the bag he goes across to his car opens the trunk throws the bag in slams the lid. He gets in the car starts up the Avenue steering around doubleparked abandoned cars stripped windowsmashed gets on the drive through the tunnel stops at Joe the Barber's for a drink leaves the car at East Third and I walks up the Avenue throwing snowballs at passing cars to East Seventh seven and three is ten

into the alley along the Frankenstein house with its ghostly turrets sinister bays the old man is in the yard hosing the statutes the statues are made of ice they're not statues they're jagged stalagmites mounds rounded caverns weird greywhite greyblack bluegray taller than the old man each time he runs the hose over them they melt freeze change he builds up an ice spire joins it with a second spire makes

a bridge a cave get out of here sonny he says dreamy every
now and then at night the kids come and break the statues.

What you doin says Nick.

Makin says the skinny old man his goat beard wobbles
when he talks.

Makin what.

Just makin.

How can I do it.

You can't sonny you're too young. You have to grow up.
Then you have to get old like me.

Can't I do it now.

No you have to wait. Get out of here sonny don't bother
me.

What do I have to do besides get old.

You have to sleep a lot. People should sleep more sonny
get out of here.

What else do I have to do.

You have to be foolish. Foolish and cranky that's important. And stubborn that's the main thing foolish cranky
and stubborn. And mean to kids he sweeps the hose around
in my direction now stop bothering me. You kids are

enough bother coming around at night breaking my things
not that I care he-he-he he chuckles to himself. First you
have to grow up very few people get that far damn few.
And then you have to be lucky like me.

How do you get to be lucky.

Well you have to try hard. And you have to be lucky.

What should I do says Nick.

First thing you should do is stop bothering me. Look
in your pockets Nick looks through his pockets.

What do you have there says the old man.

A two dollar bill says Nick a two dollar bill says the old
man see that's lucky here let me have that that's for me
what else.

A note.

What's it say.

It says expedite trail plan tonight. Upstate on the
double.

Well what are you waiting for sonny. No need to come
bothering me for anything. Now get out of here and leave
me alone he starts hosing in my direction I back out of
the yard. And get rid of that cat he yells after me. Or you'll

never grow up here are the keys he heaves a set of car keys at me what keys he's already turned back to the statues.

What keys there's a camper bus where the car was the keys fit he starts it up catches the expressway back through the tunnel around the city over the bridge out of town at the beginning of the parkway he stops for two hitchhikers a boy and a girl the girl looks the way he likes them to

look. Big eyes tits ass thin face waist belly long hair legs the boy seems a nice kid. Where you heading says Nick.

Upstate says the boy Nick pulls the camper off the road put the duffel in the back he says the girl gets in then the boy Nick pulls out I'm Nick he says.

Hi says the boy I'm Scott. This is Ova she smiles Nick stiffens Ova wears a short skirt and semitransparent white

shirt through an opening between buttons Nick can see the bottom of a tit jogging up and down with the motion of the camper.

She's my wife says the boy Nick shifts gears his hand grazes her bare thigh I don't wear a ring says Ova he doesn't own me.

We just got married says the boy how do you like it says

54

Nick.

It's great it turns you on says Ova I can see that says
Nick in the half dark of the cabin Scott and Ova are out-
lined by a glow not exactly a glow but a discontinuity of
light between their bodies and the air Ova's thigh gleams
beneath his hand on the gearshift her nipples dimple the
white cloth of her shirt we fuck all the time she says. I

hate to wear clothes I keep wanting to take them off you
don't wear many says Nick as few as possible she says.

Ova wants to make it between rides everything says the
boy it's too much it's great. We were just making it behind
those trees before you picked us up everytime Nick shifts
he grazes Ova's thigh everytime he touches her she smiles
he shifts as much as possible he's afraid to look down at his

pants it seems to Nick the cabin is filled with a pulsing
blue glow.

It's too much the way Ova turns people on says the boy.
Men women she can send out emanations I can see them
they make people sweat and quiver sometimes they light
up women pink men sort of cobalt blue wow sounds like
some kind of wild pinball machine don't it. The boy puts

his arm around Ova and begins massaging her nipple I've even seen her turning on animals. Ova rubs her thighs together Nick shifts gears his nostrils fill with the odor of raw cabbage would you like to drive for a while says Nick his hands are shaking sure thing says the boy Nick pulls over.

I'm tired he says.

So am I says Ova.

Maybe I'll go take a rest on the bed in back while Scott drives.

Hey you got a bed in back crazy says Ova.

Ova's tired says the boy.

Do you think she'd like to come back and rest with me I guess she probably would says the boy.

Ova gives Nick a push come on she says I haven't been laid out on a real bed for days maybe hours they get out climb into the back and lay down Scott starts the car Nick pulls her panties off puts them in his pocket now he says the rest of her clothes just sort of fall off of her he sticks his index finger deep into her asshole his thumb in her cunt she cries out he fills his mouth with her tit and tries to swallow it she grunts moans yells he substitutes his cock for his thumb they both come right away her yells over the roar of the camper fall apart with a moan.

After a while she feels for his face one thing about making it in a camper you can make all the noise you want she says she runs her mouth down his body and closes it over his cock they stay that way for a while then he slides into

her again this time they stay still and let the bump and sway of the camper fuck for them it takes a long time.

Time for me to drive says Nick Ova pokes her head through the curtain to the cabin we're done she tells the boy. Nick gets into the driver's seat Ova between them the boy puts his arm around her gives her a long kiss his hand under her shirt pulls her onto his lap her panties are still

in Nick's pocket he hears her groan softly she starts panting and wriggling around on the boy's lap Nick keeps his eyes on the speedometer he's going too fast he slows down in three and seven tenths miles by the odometer he hears her moan three times and gasp the boy gives a muffled dying shout. The mileage indicator reads 10737.3. She slides off his lap touches Nick lightly on his thigh and rests her head

against the boy's shoulder. Nick drives. The two kids fall
asleep smiling.

Nick pulls the camper off the road stops gets out. He walks
down the highway along the shoulder in the dark when he
sees headlights he sticks his thumb out. When there are no
headlights it's completely dark no stars he can't see the
road a yard ahead of him. It's heavy moist perfectly quiet

when a car or especially a truck is coming he can hear it
way off in the distance. He feels the presence of grass and
trees he feels it on his skin also animals. He wonders where
he's going he's a little afraid not too much just enough he
slips off his watch and heaves it into the dark. As he walks
he whistles Jor-du by Max Roach and the late Clifford
Brown he's happy it can't last. A car drives by slows pulls

onto the shoulder ahead backs up a head leans out the
right hand window where you heading says Nick.

Where it's at.

Okay he gets in they go. Fast guy accelerates to eighty
in about ten seconds keeps it there. So. What are you.

Travelling says Nick the speedometer moves to eighty-
five guy's tapping on the wheel with his ring he's way into

some rhythm.

So what are you you live around here.

No says Nick the speedometer moves to ninety.

So what are you you up at the college I can drop you at the college.

Okay says Nick.

So what are you hitchhiking.

Looks like says Nick.

So what are you you can't afford a bus ticket.

Don't like busses says Nick.

You guys. He keeps it right at ninety for five minutes. tapping the wheel then starts letting it down eighty-five seventy-five seventy-four seventy-three he turns to Nick. So what are you he says.

What do you mean says Nick.

So you're Carl says the guy.

What makes you think I'm Carl.

I got a thing with names I never get em wrong.

That's remarkable.

Yeah ainit. Well glad to know you Carl my name's Nick a terrifying yowl tears out of the back of the car my god what's that says Carl.

Nothing I got a cat in the trunk says Nick he touches a switch a soul thudding rock number buzzes Carl's eardrums ah heard it through the grape vine ah heard it through the grape vine.

Open the glove compartment Nick yells Carl opens it you wanna take out that baggie in there Carl takes it out

unroll it Nick yells Carl unrolls it it's filled with skinny little cigarettes you wanna hand me one of those joints yells Nick Carl hands it to him.

Thanks yells Nick open the glove compartment you see that wallet in there yells Nick you wanna take it out Carl takes it out. Open it up yells Nick Carl opens it up you see that badge in there yells Nick yeah yells Carl you're

under arrest yells Nick I'm a narcotics agent you just gave me a marijuana cigarette he turns off the music I'll bet you're surprised.

Stunned.

Open the glove compartment.

What now.

You see those handcuffs in there.

I see a gun.

Not the gun the handcuffs.

Hey is this a real gun Carl takes it out of the glove compartment.

Not the gun dummy the handcuffs says Nick.

Is it real.

No Carl opens the window and pulls the trigger the

gun jumps in his hand there's a loud bang.

It's got blanks says Nick Carl closes the window and pulls the trigger there's a deafening noise the window turns into a spiderweb with a hole in the middle.

I know who you are says Carl. You're Tommy the Tourist.

You just make that up.

Carl pokes the gun into Tommy's ribs you're not safe you know that.

Why not.

Travelling around trapping guys like that you're getting less safe every minute.

How.

Guys like you stop the car. People are getting sore.

You're not going to kill me are you.

No stop the car Tommy stops the car I'm not Tommy he says.

Get out they get out and walk into a field you're not going to kill me are you says Tommy no keep walking they reach some bushes.

Lie down says Carl. On your belly Tommy lies down.

I'm going to kill you says Carl.

Oh no.

Yep.

You said you wouldn't.

I was lying.

I'm not Tommy.

I don't care who you are Tommy I'm going to kill you.

You're a liar. I'm going to kill you for lying.

All right I'm Tommy.

Tommy the Tourist.

Tommy the Tourist. Don't kill me.

Say please.

Please.

Please what.

Please don't kill me.

Why not.

I told you the truth.

I was just trying to find out if you're Tommy. If you weren't Tommy I wouldn't kill you but now that I know you're Tommy I'm going to kill you. Ready.

I'm not Tommy.

There you go again. Ready.

Please don't.

Shut up how would you like it a bullet in the head or would you rather I crush your skull with the gun butt.

Bullet.

Carl slams the gun butt down as hard as he can on Tommy's head then goes back to the car. He throws the

gun into some bushes pukes two or three times starts the car lights a joint pulls out accelerating fast. The cat yowls. He turns on the music taps fingers on steering wheel in rhythm music off still tapping slightly high comes to a town up a hill bricked roads elms close in over head small groups going up and down couples three and four boys trees thicken leaves yellowing towers turrets arches groups

carrying school books straggling along walks stone gate
long rolling lawn brick slate greenery crowds of disconsolate children adolescents clump disperse circulate now
and then one starts to shake his body a spasm of some
kind a dance the beginning of a violent act then stops.
He pulls up in front of a monstrosity in late Neogoth
walks into the great hall goes over to a table marked Infor-

mation say where can I score a nickel of something he says.

We don't do that here try the Rathskellar downstairs
she says like very cool.

Thanks hey when ya get offa work.

Don't be funny. He goes downstairs the Rathskellar is
crowded beer jukebox he looks around sits down next to
some kids talking politics writes out a note it says let's

trash the nuclear reactor he passes it to one of the kids.

Weird says the kid.

Didn't we do that once already today so what's the joke
says another.

No like I just got into town I'm looking to crash.

Try the Howard Johnson.

Cool where can I find some soft pussy.

Did you try the information table.

Yeah but she says hers ain't soft hey would like to score some good grass.

How much.

A nickel an ounce it's a sale.

How come.

I'm relocating.

Where.

Canada it's too drafty this side of Niagara.

What did you burn your 2S.

I graduated I'm a little older.

Worst fucking mistake you ever made what are you about twenty-two.

Way off twenty-four.

There were some people who wanted to buy a few hours ago they're over at a crash pad.

7310 College Avenue.

How did you know.

The grapevine.

You Tommy.

Yeah.

They were looking for you.

Well they've almost found me Tommy goes back to the car heads for College Avenue knocks at 7310.

Who a kid's voice.

Tommy.

Come Tommy walks in.

Did you come says the kid.

Don't I look it.

Are you Tommy says the kid.

Why not hi says Tommy to a very nice looking chick.

Can I have my panties back now she says.

Not yet I hear you can sell me some grass says Tommy.

I hear you're selling you kidding says the kid.

I'm kidding a nickel an ounce says Tommy.

How come so cheap.

Volume try a joint he rolls one they pass it around a few times okay says the kid here's the bread. Tommy hands him the bag I'm Donald says the kid I guess you know Trixie.

No I just happen to be carrying her panties around in my pocket how about another joint.

Sure the kid rolls a joint passes it to Tommy Tommy

takes out his wallet shows his badge I'm a narcotics agent
you're under arrest. The both of yiz. Here's your panties.

What for you kidding.

For giving me a marijuana cigarette.

I mean you're not serious.

Don't I look serious come on we're going down to the
station is that serious.

Well like okay far out I mean look like jesus I mean oh
wow like off the wall baby.

Let's go.

Like wait a minute you know I mean let's cool it I mean
can't we work something out.

Yeah I guess we could work something out.

Like what man I mean anything.

Like let me fuck your girlfriend. For a couple of days.

I can't.

Why not.

She's not my girlfriend.

Well who is your girlfriend.

She'll be here in a few minutes.

Is she nice.

Well I like her.

In a few minutes Velma walks in this is Tommy he's a narcotics agent he's going to arrest us unless you fuck him says Donald.

Are you being funny says Velma.

It's for real baby says Donald Tommy rattles his handcuffs.

Are you being funny says Velma Tommy reaches for her ass she sidesteps don't get funny with me says Velma.

Come on Velma says Donald he takes her hand and tries to give it to Tommy she pulls away I don't think this is very funny she says is everyone getting funny.

All right let's go says Tommy he moves to the door wait a minute she thinks we're being funny says Donald look

says Donald this is serious he's going to take us to jail right now. If you don't fuck him.

How many times says Velma.

For a couple of days.

For a couple of days that's too long I haven't got time for that there's been another tongue job.

Another tongue job how do you know.

I work for Information.
Where.
President's house. They're sitting in they've got it locked up.
Who told you.
President. Nick's on the ledge.
How'd he get through.

He's in drag. Harrold's with him they've got dynamite.
Christ let's get over there before it explodes they run out-side up College Avenue to the campus they hear a barrage of gunshots already they can smell teargas when they get there it's still going they push into the crowd behind the barricades police firing handguns rifles they're blanks some-body says a kid stumbles out the front door holding his

stomach he falls down the steps the shooting stops. They come out one by one stripped to their underpants hands over head coughing bleeding tears pouring down their faces those who can walk helping those who can't one kid sneezes as he comes out the door a shot he falls headfirst on the stairs the crowd instantly silent silence between break-ing waves why'd you do that comes a voice.

He flinched I thought it was blanks jesus I killed a kid the wave breaks someone screams a girl runs over to the kid on the steps the wooden barricades go over Toro comes out of the building onto the steps beret and fatigues holding his hands up for quiet.

The pigs are murdering us he says. They're cutting our tongues out one by one. You're next. Get a gun he's sur-

rounded by police billy clubs flashing up and down blood puddling between swinging boots drools down steps they don't stop it goes on and on come on says Donald.

Where says Trixie.

The Professor.

Who's the Professor says Tommy.

He's an inside agitator they drive into an elm laned sub-

urb stop in a nouveau Tudor development the Professor opens the door.

I saw it on television he says.

What can we do.

The Professor strokes his beard I know how badly you want to do something but he strokes there's nothing you can do nothing nothing no salvation I've thought about it.

What then.

What then is mazol.

What's mazol.

Mazol is as mazol does. When you find something that's mazol not the thing but the finding. And sometimes it's losing but not often it's often hard to say. If you don't know I can't tell you if you do I don't need to he turns on the

television they're still beating Toro the clubs the boots you can't see him blood sheets down the steps he turns it off.

The Professor shakes his head there's nothing you can do. Not till you get it together.

How do we do that.

Start over he begins to sing in a high creaky voice.

Girls love a man with mazol

Everyone's his fan

But does the man make the mazol

Or does the mazol make the man.

He repeats doing a little jig. I don't get it says Velma.

Take risks don't hold your tongue for example speak before you think says the Professor. He reaches into the air plucks a firecracker from nothingness it disappears which hand he says.

Left says Trixie the Professor smiles the firecracker emerges red between his thick lips fuse burning he throws it into the air it explodes he pulls it out of his ear holds it up dynamite says the Professor.

You're a very strange cat says Tommy.

Everybody's getting funny says Velma.

I'm sorry I can't help you. You have to get it together says the Professor they leave he shuts the door opens it calls down the lawn.

See Frank Stein.

Who's he.

He gets it together the Professor shuts the door they go back to campus Toro is lying on the steps half conscious

bloody they can hear him trying to breathe it sounds like e-e-e-E-E-E e-e-E-E-E e-E-E-E-E they didn't even arrest him Velma takes his head on her lap he's dying she says his eyes flutter open his mouth gapes blood comes out he gestures finger pointing to mouth they bend close. It sounds like waiter . . . suck . . . meet or maybe traitor . . . luck . . . bleed or maybe sailor . . . duck . . . sneeze. His eyes jell his mouth sags his head falls to one side. It's not Toro says Velma. It's Jojo.

Someone comes out of the building it's the President Nick's on the stairs in drag Harrold comes from behind a hedge it's a meet. Everyone takes out his stick of dynamite. Are you Nixon asks Tommy Nick takes off his long blond wig steps out of his dress you're not supposed to ask that

says Nick I'm in drag so am I says the President he unloosens his flowing hair takes off his suit jacket undoes his tie unbuttons his shirt down between his bobbing breasts you're Nixie says Carl. Where's Toro says Velma I'm Toro says Tommy my cover is bull Rex drives up in the car with Ova steps out puts his arm around her we're going to take you home he says say goodbye to your friends the motor

still running the cat yowls Rex takes out his long trunk key don't open that he puts it in jiggles it it doesn't work it works the cat yowls the bag is alive he lets it out the eye a puff of charcoal with an eye traced on it alive alive unbelievable starved it's not so bad I pick it up stroke its fur it shivers in my arms lick its eye it feels rough almost vomit put back in bag tie top put bag in front of car tire get in start car roll slowly in first over bag stop Rex holds up the bloody bag this is yours the final find throws it through window onto front seat a siren starts rises falls rises rises.

6

A big dog is licking Carl's eyes he opens them it's the sun he rolls over stretches out his hand to the damp grass next to his cheek squirms out of his bag it's late he gets out the map the siren keeps rising it's too high for Carl to hear beyond a wire fence cows graze he walks to the highway. After a while a camper stops two kids inside a boy and a

girl Carl gets in next to the girl where you headin says the boy west says Carl.
How far.
Far as I can.
Where you start.
I forget.

74

Off the wall says the boy I'm Scott this is Ova we just got married.

He doesn't own me says Ova.

That's good says Carl her foot keeps getting in the way when he tries to stretch his legs Ova is restless squirming around in her seat she sort of smells funny.

That's why we look kinda like sleepy we don't get much sleep says the boy he gags no it's a chuckle we fuck all the time says Ova each other other people she wears a semi-transparent white shirt shortest possible miniskirt Carl wonders when he's going to get breakfast have you had breakfast yet says Carl.

I'm tired says Ova she squirms stretches rests her head on Carl's shoulder he opens his window low green hills sunny quiet still.

It's great being married it turns you on you married says the boy.

I'm hungry says Carl.

Like it's too much the way Ova turns people on it turns me on I mean she does that to everybody I mean like don't worry if she turns you on.

Why not.

Why not well I mean you can fuck her if you want to you want to fuck her.

I have to take a shit maybe after that says Carl.

You're an uptight cat you know that says the boy.

Don't start that he has to take a shit can't you see he has to take a shit says Ova.

Well that's just it he has to take a shit why didn't he take a shit before he got in here I mean I didn't ask for his shit.

Well he didn't ask for your shit.

Well I didn't ask for yours.

Why didn't you.

I don't ask. If somebody wants to give it to me all right I don't ask.

Look who's talking uptight. When we got married you

said you were going to find me other men to fuck I suppose
that was just big talk. Already you're breaking your promises you don't love me anymore tears dribble down the
sides of her nose.

So what's the matter with him. I pick up a guy off the
side of the road I practically tell him to fuck you what do

you want me to do unzip his fly I mean there's a limit to
what I can do. Trouble with you is you don't like to fuck
enough.

What are you saying I love it. I love it. There's nobody
who loves it more than me.

Yes there is.

Who.

My last wife she was a bitch of an old lady but she sure
liked to fuck. Only she was possessive you know what I
mean possessive I can't stand that.

Do you think we should get a divorce says Ova.

Again what for. What good would it do. The divorce I

want is a bigger divorce than you can give me that's what we all want isn't it.

What are we going to do.

Drive.

I feel like a desert inside says Ova. There's nothing there but the wind that sweeps it away. Do you think that means

I want to die.

Trust the wind says Scott.

I wish I could feel empty like Ova says Carl. A smart old man once told me what's wrong with me he said I think too much he said don't think talk. Don't talk do. Then don't do. Do you understand what that means.

No says Scott.

I can't explain what I feel inside but it's very painful it's like somebody I love has died. Me. If I were driving I'd floor the gas pedal and drive off the road says Carl.

Do you want to drive says Scott.

I want to say something right now and that is I love you

both very much says Carl. Especially Ova but both of you. And I also want to say something else. I wish very much that Eleanor Roosevelt were still alive at that he begins to cry for some reason it also makes the other two cry Scott pulls over to the side of the road after a while he and Ova stop crying Carl doesn't stop what's the matter says Ova.

I have to go to the bathroom quavers Carl.
Carl can I ask you something seriously.
What's that Scott.
Did you have infantile paralysis.
Yes.
So did I they both start crying again so does Ova. What

are you crying about says Scott.
I still have it says Ova they each take one of her hands sit that way for a while I have to say something says Scott.
What's that Scott says Carl.
I can't go on. I can't do it another day. I mean every morning I wake up and start driving it's the same god

damn thing day in and day out what's the point. I can't go
on driving myself this way what's it all add up to.

Cool it it's all a trip says Carl.

That's easy for you to say you just started says Scott.

You think that's easy for me to say that's not easy for me
to say.

No why not.

Why not because I stink. Worse than that I'm no good
at all I'm garbage shit phony all lies says Carl.

That's not true you're a big bad man says Ova.

It's all show I know what I'm like. Not worth spitting on
not worth scraping off the sole of your shoe. All fake fake

heart fake guts fake balls oh my god I'm so ashamed of
myself I'm so worthless.

You. Me. Me says Scott I'm the one who's worthless. I'm
so worthless it's unfathomable. I'm so empty I don't even
know there's anything missing. At least you're not a Wasp.

I eat you up Carl says Ova.

I'm scared wails Carl.

Of what.

I'm going to disappear help. Oh god hold on to me.

You're putting me on says Scott Ova starts fingering his penis you're my big bad man says Ova.

I'm little.

You're getting bigger.

You're right I am getting bigger wow. I'm not really so bad though.

You're a shit. Don't give me that nice crap I know you you think you can shit all over me you prick well you can't.

Cunt. Who do you think you're talking to. Get in the

back.

What about him.

He can sit here and jerk off come on move Carl pulls her out of the cabin shoves her into the back of the camper and unzips his fly suck it he says. That's enough he says after a while she comes up he busts her right in the mouth she bounces off the wall of the camper blood on her chin.

What's that for she says holding her lip you forgot to say thank you he says take your clothes off I oughta walk right outa here.

Oh please no she strips polish my boot he says she comes down on his boot slides back and forth around please she

says he puts the sole of his boot on her tit shoves her down goes in she starts coming right away I love you she says.

More than your husband.

Much more your cock's bigger the spasm rises from her gut she comes grunting and snorting like a pig in shit.

You done she says.

Yeah I guess so.

How about getting your cock out of me he gets off her she puts her clothes back on he follows her back to the cabin. Done says Scott.

Yeah says Ova.

How was it.

He's disgusting. You should have seen the loathsome
things he made me do Carl reaches for the door handle.
Where you going says Ova she locks the door.

I said where do you think you're going says Ova. Carl
can't answer.

Smatter cat gotcha tongue. You're loathsome. You're

beneath contempt. You're a piece of shit.

Carl can't talk.

Wyncha say something. You don't even exist.

Carl opens his mouth but nothing comes out.

Bet he's some kinda kike says Scott.

Or worse says Ova let's go the camper disappears in a

cloud of dust. Carl falls down on the side of the road and
has an attack he clutches at his throat things are starting to
happen too fast for me he thinks to himself.

A bus pulls up maybe this is a bus stop Carl thinks out
gets a short fellow with slightly hunched shoulders soft
bushy moustache immigrant teeth he looks like a tramp.

84

Mam mamia he says he bends over Carl feels his brow takes his pulse watsa da mat he says Carl points to his throat starts panting and gagging the fellow turns to the bus yoohoo he yodels two more fellows come out bearded they're dressed like tramps or refugees or gypsies you takee thisee boy chop chop innee bus he says they take him

inside lay him across a seat the bus pulls away Carl claws at his throat what's with him Uncle Schmuck says one of the fellows. Uncle Schmuck points to his head kishkas he says he looks down at Carl with glittering charisma eyes. Mine share loco zees nowt yolk dah best ben doin what I tellya. Open you cottonpickin mouth out mit der tongue.

Fairthur mi bye fairthur o so eggsellant. Now say ah. Something like a death rattle comes out of Carl's throat followed by gagging he begins to hiccup Uncle Schmuck grabs his throat squeezes shakes Carl lets out a series of henny squeaks tray bueno says Uncle Schmuck go on cuk cuk cuk says Carl cuk-cuk-cuk-a-doo cuk-a-doo cuk-cuk-a-

doo cuk-a-do-o-o-o-o Carl is really into it cuk-a-do-o-o-o-o
Aunt Poopik says Uncle Schmuck a big busty manmother
of a woman comes up from the back of the bus vus vilsta
she says kvick says Uncle Schmuck take his temperature
they unzip his pants reach in cuk cuk cuk goes Carl they
work inside his pants he starts wheezing and gasping coughs

his breathing is deeper his pulse improving now outski
vit el tonk says Schmuck say ah ah says Carl louder a-a-
ah louder AAAH AH AAAAAAH AAAAAAAAAAA
ekco ekco says Schmuck he pulls down Carl's pants Aunt
Poopik grabs his cock squeezes licks it sticks a thermometer
up his ass a-a-A-A-a-ah goes Carl his breathing is good his

color is good his pulse is good Frank takes the thermometer
out looks at it you're okay fella okay auntie that's it Aunt
Poopik lets his cock fall out of her mouth Carl sits straight
up stares around wildly more he says.

Ah-hah says Uncle Schmuck now he can talk. What do
you have to say for yourself chum.

Carl blinks looks around one small step for man and a giant step for mankind he says he collapses back across the seat and falls into a deep sleep.

While Carl is asleep he dreams he's Henry Aldrich he dreams Henry Aldrich wakes up in a silver Cadillac at a gas station on the Indiana Thruway the gas station is

named Booth Tarkington. The attendant comes to the window asks how much fill it up says Uncle Schmuk only now he's named Uncle Don check the oil and water look at the battery test the air pressure and get the windshield. Uncle Don turns takes Henry's pulse how are you son he says his moustache is gone and his teeth are a lot better.

I dreamed there was a guy and a girl in a camper says Henry.

Fellow with a square jaw and albino eyelids. Travels with a blue eyed round faced girl also blond. Heck. That was no dream that was the White Asp and Mary.

Uncle Don I want to thank you for all you've done for

me.

Gee whiz I'd do the same for anybody. How're you feeling.

Good but a little lonely.

Lonely you can have Siss Siss he yells slim trim Siss pops up in the back seat what is it Uncle Don Uncle Don pats

her on the bottom honey I'm giving you to this nice boy for a while I want you to show him a nice time he can use it. Hi hon says Siss she slips over the seat sits next to Henry.

Uncle Don says Henry I have two questions.

You're only supposed to get one.

Well they're connected.

Okay shoot.

The first question is my life is empty and my work has no meaning what should I do.

That's all what else.

What's the meaning of this trip.

Uncle Don ponders a minute let's go outside to Booth

88

Tarkington he says. They stroll around Booth Tarkington
Uncle Don steers Henry by his arm Booth Tarkington has
a great deal of civic pride he says. Among other things
they lay claim to the world's most beautiful gas pumps
Henry examines them they are beautiful so much so Henry
feels that he wouldn't really believe it if this weren't a

dream he notes their subtle pastels the brilliant liquatex
hues the everchanging display of colored lights the neon
trim the rocketship motif emphasized with strips of chrome
the elaborate dials the tubing the gurgling liquids the bells
the eight varieties the heraldry of the trademark and liter-
ally above all the giant sign higher than the trees higher

than the hills brighter than the moon. Frank flicks a gilt
hose see that ain't no cherry phosphate they got comin
outa there nope. This ain't your ordinary corner drug-
store. Nosirree this here's what I'd call a shrine why people
come to Booth Tarkington from all over the country you
know that as well as I. What do they find here well shucks

I guess everybody finds something different but most of em find gas. Now you see what the meter on this here pump reads it reads 17 point 3 gallons 7 dollars 33 cents that's the answer to your first question it's in code. A code that when broken is utterly meaningless. I don't understand says Henry you don't have to understand everything

says Uncle Don he hands Henry a road map and here's the answer to your second question. Think sideways. Now here's the answer to a question you haven't even thought of yet the magic syllable. The magic syllable is oi take a deep breath and repeat with me. Oi-i-i. Breathe. Oi-i-i. Breathe. Oi-i-i. That's right now at least you're breathing

it's a sign of life. Now close your eyes and think about it as you say it o i o i o i concentrate keep your eyes closed say it by yourself as long as you can oi-i-i oi-i-i oi-i-i-i-i-i as he dreams he falls asleep he hears Uncle Don say that oughta hold the little schmuck for a while.

When he wakes up he can't remember anything even

his name it's weird he's not even surprised. To his right
there's a field to his left a highway around him a ditch
above the sky. Blue a few white clouds. He tries his body
it works nothing sore in fact he feels terrific. A little horny
maybe he rubs his cock still there old snake lifts its head
inquisitive then goes back to sleep. He wonders who he is

it doesn't matter it's all geometry what does that mean.
Actually he's a nonentity a vacuum a campground of con-
flicting tribes in uneasy truce that's what it means.
It means angles and velocities and effects of effects of effects
of effects it means luck he feels light buoyant he can't
remember anything what a relief. He looks through his

pockets nothing there something there a road map of the
states something else a crumpled piece of paper with three
words scrawled in pencil

> empty
> fox
> speeds

right on he thinks to himself if you're empty and you're smart you keep moving. Fast he gets up climbs out of the ditch he remembers something he remembers something a siren. No not remember he hears it but only in his head he remembers nothing. He looks at the map. Near as he can figure he's close to a place called Belvidere on top of

a low hill. The land seems wider here opens and flattens out. Wider than what he doesn't know image of a city mountains close hills wide water. I love you. Words in his head. My head. Floods slides plague reports in the southwest. Tired of comedy. High winds across the prairie a storm front from Canada. His first ride is a salesman he

keeps the radio turned to the news. Explosions fires. Plague reports in the southwest. Around them the corn is dying they hit miles and miles of yellowing brown wilted stalks. He gets off at a gas station in a place called Black Earth a girl comes up to him he loves her.

I'm in a hurry she says.

Me too.

Good can you drive.

Sure I can drive he's pretty sure he can drive let's go she says they get in her bug I'll go till I'm tired she says. She drives. Fast and intensely without talking at Tomah they change places still without saying anything to one another

he can drive. At La Crosse they stop for lunch still no talking when they cross the Mississippi he asks her name she looks at the map for a while picks a town. Alma she says what's yours.

Rex.

Do you want me to drive yet Rex.

I'll take it to the other side of the river they've been crossing the river for about a half an hour already it seems Alma he says I have something to tell you.

I know it I don't want to talk about it.

I love you.

I don't want to talk about it.

What do you want to talk about.

I don't want to talk about anything I want to drive.

Across the Mississippi the land is less amusing it seems to Rex. The dying corn is the same only there's more of it and more of it is dying. And there are these long uncooperative stretches of pure distance naked to the eye and to

the wind rising across their widths ripping through occasional islands of cottonwoods way off to make the bug lurch and shudder when a wave of it hits. Everything is more serious here they stop for coffee in Rochester home of the famous clinic that's been trying to cure us for years it gains stature and loses ground every day.

By sunset his love is hopeless desperate. He knows that she's a fugitive doomed that she's committed some definitive act planted a bomb participated in an abduction acted as an accomplice in a bank robbery where a guard was killed or if she hasn't already done it is about to do it. She refuses to talk or allow him to talk he knows by osmosis by sitting next to her attending her silence isolation. Or maybe she's the blank page on which Rex writes his story maybe its Rex who's done all that he isn't sure it doesn't matter either way he's frightened the news speaks of road blocks. There's been an escalation of the latest deescalation intensifying protest thereby increasing backlash.

Harassment seems standard procedure passports checked at every tollbooth contraband searches become beatings and rapes pacifists found murdered on back roads noone under twenty-one or black can travel by airplane. An army of agents has infiltrated everything there are provocateurs double-agents triple-agents noone can any longer distin-

guish plot from counterplot even the agencies. Everybody by now is either spy or counterspy it doesn't matter which at least that's Rex's opinion the important thing is don't trust anybody. Even if you love them. Even yourself. Above all don't talk don't say anything it can only be used against you. Besides it won't help it's hopeless. Unless you have the power that's what frightens Rex most he thinks he might have it. That's why he sweats and shakes next to her as if he can't contain what's surging through him as they approach a place called Blue Earth looking for a motel for the night.

That night they stay at a place called The Vacancy

Motel out in the flatness near Blue Earth which they never see that is they see the earth but not the town big hard clods of it blucblack out of which the grow rows and rows of rustling brown stunted useless corn at the edge of which on the flatness in the winds sweeping toward them out of the immense fields and then away and then another wave

toward them again they lock the door behind them in The Vacancy Motel. As soon as they put their things down he grabs her and tries to give her a kiss she shoves him away.

Alma he says all right she says. If we have to blabber here it is. Three weeks ago I was gang raped by a bunch of hardhats what about it.

How many says Rex.
Ten.
That's quite a few.
Damn right so ever since then I'm not fucking anybody.
Even me.
That's right sonny.

Well. I guess I can understand that.
I doubt it.
I mean that's really tough luck I mean it must have been
awful I mean . . .
Shut your ass.
What.

You heard me buster shut your ass.
What.
I mean don't talk when you don't know willya.
Okay sorry.
Okay sorry she sneers she lays down on the bed and closes
her eyes.

What was it like says Rex.

You really like to blabber don't you.

You don't have to tell me if you don't want to.

I'll tell you. They said take off your clothes girlie you're going to get fucked so I took off my clothes and I got fucked.

And that was it.

All sorts of ways I didn't have much choice. I never got fucked so many ways before. Or so many times. They just told me what to do and I did it I didn't have much choice.

It must have been awful.

I kept having orgasms. I didn't want to I couldn't help

it. I COULDN'T HELP IT. I wanted to. I never had so many organsms. I tried to imagine it was my boyfriend then later after it was over when I was with my boyfriend I tried to imagine it was the hardhats. So I got scared and I'm not fucking anybody anymore that includes you buster so don't get any ideas.

I'm sorry Alma but you've got to fuck me.

I've got to who do you think you are Wonder Wart Hog
or something.

I've got the power.

The what.

I've got the POWER.

What are you trying to freak me out.

Rex reaches down into his pants and pulls out his stick
of dynamite I'm it he says he holds it up.

You're it.

I'm it.

So. You're it.

That's right so don't fuck around with me or I'm liable
to blow us both up. Once my fuse is lit it's out of my hands.

So you think you're it she reaches down her dress pulls
out her stick of dynamite I'm it.

Rex goes pale. You're it then he says this is it he takes
out his matches. You want to go first.

You go first says Alma Rex lights his fuse shuts his eyes tight puts his free finger in his ear.

Tell me a little bit about yourself says Alma. How did a nice boy like you end up this way. Where did we fail you.

Rex opens his eyes when the fuse is lit history cancels out he says he puts the dynamite in his mouth his other finger

in his other ear his eyes focus on the fuse as it burns shorter they grow larger larger more crossed they're bulging out of his head BANG. The dynamite goes off like a trick cigar Rex falls to the floor.

Rex screams Alma. Rex. Rex Rex Rex Rex she's all over him kissing him hugging him feeling his heart his brow

taking his pulse rubbing his dick Rex opens his eyes wipes a little soot off his face that's all he asks.

I love you says Alma.

Your turn undress says Rex she takes her clothes off lies down on the bed.

You're it you know the rules says Rex Alma nods Rex

lights her dynamite imagine it's the hardhats says Rex he sticks the end up her vagina Alma groans shuts her eyes lies frozen how did we get into this says Rex. Why are we here. Why are we doing this to ourselves. What's the point of it all.

Data accumulates obscurity persists says Alma the fuse

burns down to the dynamite there's an instant's pause then a sizzling sound they look at one another wide-eyed.

A dud whispers Rex a DUD. It's a new world.

Now we can settle down get married and lead happy normal lives says Alma she takes the dynamite out of her cunt.

Get dressed we're going to find a justice of the peace says

Rex they leave get married go shopping in the supermarket come back with paper bags full of good things to eat.

You put the stuff away dear I'll start cooking says Alma.

What are we having for dinner says Rex.

Tongue.

Tongue.

Yes I think of it as your tongue. I love tongue there's something so male about it what do you suppose that is they tickle one another.

How do you cook it says Rex.

Take the tongue says Alma. Boil a pot of water put it in. Add a bouquet garni of marjoram thyme basil and bay

leaf. Allow simmer. Prepare three medium onions whole two large carrots four stalks celery with leaves seven and a half sprigs parsley eight peppercorns and at the right moment pop them into the pot. Allow simmer. Consult the stars and jab occasionally with fork when it stops flinching remove from fire immerse in icy water for thirty seconds

peel and trim. Do not remove the schlung repeat do not remove the schlung. Return to boiling water briefly. Carve and serve.

Sounds scrumchy dear.

She wiggles her shoulders and after dinner you know what.

102

What.

Make bunnies.

Ah hah hah.

He reads the paper she cooks when it's done she carves starting with the very tip the first incision is the circumcision she sings gaily she slips it onto his plate. Followed

by some nice firm red middle slices he pounds the table.

What is this I want the schlung.

You can't have it it's too fatty and gristly and disgusting and nitty gritty with all them little veins and shit ugh.

Don't hand me that I want the schlung.

It's not good for you.

Fuck off give it to me or I'll shove a carrot up your ass.

I put it down the Dispos-all here she shoves some tongue into his mouth isn't that delicious.

Um you're right it is delicious can I have some more.

They eat tongue. They eat and they eat. They eat tongue till they're helpless till tongue is coming out their assholes

they eat tongue till they can't talk anymore then they make
bunnies.

Should I take off my clothes now says Alma.

Yeah I guess so (urp).

She takes off her clothes unzips his fly pulls down his
pants jumps into bed spreads her legs wide gaping let's go

Wonder Wart Hog she says sock it to me.

He stands there with his pants around his ankles like I'm
too full.

Whaddyamean too full feed me some a that raunchy old
schlung baby I'm hungry.

Don't be so aggressive.

Who's aggressive come on ram that dynamite up my cunt
and light the fuse.

What is this Sadie Hawkins Day.

So whatsa matter with Sadie Hawkins Day that put you
uptight.

Are you gonna start with the woman's lib rap.

Can't take it huh. Big dong can't take woman's lib. Can't get his weenie up. Thinks he's a dude but he's just a dud. I know your game buster you thought you were escaping. You thought you were going to club your way out with your cock. You're a fugitive. What's your real name Rex.

I don't have a real name.

I ought to turn you in. A fugitive and no real name but I'm not you're lucky. I'm sending you to a meet you have to deliver a message this is the message. Speed increases space expands repeat.

Speed increases space expands what's your real name.

Nada.

Then you are it.

I was it before your greatgrandmother met your great-grandfather now I disappear she walks to the door now you're it.

Wait where's the meet.

In Mitchell ask for Mitch she disappears. Rex lies down

to think about it takes notes. What now Rex wonders what next he closes his notebook his eyes tired of simulation how did I get into this I allow his mind to wander play with possibilities he daydreams he's lying I'm lying in the sun on a chaise inventing stories about himself above a blue ocean bougainvillaea eucalyptus jacaranda blue sky white

ships sail by there's an undefined loud noise and an ellipsis his reality comes down on him with the force of an overhead garage door coming down on his head I've been hit he thinks I think I'm not even surprised beware of head wounds expect the unexpected speed increases I get up he can get up discover I'm bleeding he's bleeding. Profusely.

Blood on glasses notebook blood running down cheek blood coming out of mouth tongue must have bitten tongue so that's it. Could have bitten my tongue off a bee stings his arm. Tetanus says the man in the white coat. You shouldn't worry.

Where am I.

Up shit's creek mein schatz. He's a short man slightly hunched shoulders black beard charismatic eyes.

Who are you.

I'm Mitch but my real name you should know is Frank Stein. Doctor Frank Stein. Who you.

I don't know.

There's your first problem sonny I want to see your license and registration.

I lost them what are you going to do with me.

Vay if I tell you you'll plotz.

What is this place he looks around at the Turco-Romanesque decor the strange mosaics out of *The Wonderland of*

Knowledge 1939 this is an old castle says Frank chust like in the old days mit Boris. Only it's made completely out of corn. Barbaric so much of our work here lacks conviction he sighs zo mach schnell the storm comes. We need information from you schatzie.

What information.

Your life story.

I forgot it.

Make it up shtunk. And no lies remember this is the Corn Palace. The walls have ears.

It must be a maize.

That's the kernel of it. Zo. Hurry up don't try to tell the

whole thing at once do it part by part the story of your head the story of your legs the story of your cock. Start with the heart for example tell me the story of your heart do you know your heart has a memory.

My heart doesn't remember anything.

Putz. Make it up it's the same thing.

I don't want to remember anything I want to be numb and ruthless. And beautiful.

Patty. Laverne. Two blonds in lab coats come in what is it Frankie they say in unison. Pull down his pants and get the electrodes oh my god he thinks to himself they're going to take my temperature he struggles against the

straps holding him down they're going to get inside wait
he says.

Ready to talk go on.

I can't remember anything.

Make it up Stein hands him a pad of paper make it up
it's a confession no lies Maxine faster Maxine rolls in a

bank of electronic equipment dials lights coils beeps Patty
attaches an electrode to his penis Laverne one to his tongue
Stein gives him an electrographic pencil plugs it in it's
simple as long as you're writing nothing happens as soon
as you stop a mounting current of electricity is sent through
your body growing in strength with the length of the pause

for example the character on the table shrieks his body jerks
zo get the message the first question is write an essay on
your heart my heart he writes shriek my heart my heart the
story of my heart is the story of my life shriek my heart
dilates and contracts shriek my heart shriek my heart aches
a drowsy numbness dulls my sense I think I'm having a

heart attack have a heart home is where the heart is shriek
my heart is my basso continuo imitation of my heart thung-
CHUNG thung-CHUNG can't write prolonged shriek a
history of my heart when I was a boy thung-CHUNG when
I was a child thung-CHUNG when I was a fetus thung-
CHUNG thung-CHUNG pulsation plasma protoplasm in-

out thung-CHUNG all things provided all in those days I
was a fish worm amoeba thung-CHUNG dilations contrac-
tions can't write prolonged shriek all things provided all
in those days open-close thung-CHUNG open-close my
heart was open it took it took gave back what it had de-
manding and generous beggar and prince open-close then

the revolution as he writes he gulps air like a fish lips
protruding neck laboring like gills his body squirms
wriggles undulates a great worm with a head and a notebook on its chest everything was turned upsidedown I
don't know when this happened apparently I did something wrong there wasn't enough of anything or so they

said when you wanted something you had to make out papers I became stingy and brilliant I shone like a diamond I was closed as an ax-edge then I was king but it didn't matter I wasn't loved his chest heaves again again a sob tears through his throat the notebook falls to the floor my heart prolonged shriek his body jerks he clutches his

chest Stein replaces the notebook am I dying he writes adjectives applying to my heart black dried tiny prune coal cinder clinker terror petrified brittle bursting can't write I'm dying shriek shriek prolonged shriek prolonged shriek endless weird despairing terrified heart rending shriek accompanied by convulsions streaming tears green vomity

drool he curls up like a foetus uncoils with a snap into back arch on head and heels erect penis shooting great gouts of sperm into the air coil uncoil repeat repeat half repeat collapse smell of shit as his bowels void silence. Frank Stein undoes the straps goes to the sink washes his hands gets out his doctor kit softly hums to himself

Cook a goulash
Bake a cake
From these parts
A man I make
he puts his hand to the cold immobile chest the wet icy
brow lifts an eyelid and looks in with a flashlight applies a

stethoscope thumps the chest a flicker animates the face
or is it his imagination Frank freezes almost stops breathing
as if there were only air enough in the lab for one of them
a strange sound comes from the body on the table. A kind
of spastic panting sort of like a baby starting to stir and
without fully waking just beginning to cry ah ah ah-huh

ah-huh a movement flicks across the face this time no
mistaking the left eyelid begins to flutter the lips move a
bit a horrible twitching starts first in one part of the face
then another the left cheek goes into an awful spastic
convulsion the eyes begin to blink ah ah ah-huh ah-huh
aah aaah aaaah CHOO the sneeze jerks his trunk forward

almost upright then he falls back gesundheit says Frank.
    I'm dead says the body on the table.
    He lives cries Frank.
    Oh god I'm a corpse.
    He lives he lives.
    Dead dead says the corpse.

    He lives he speaks. A real mensch yet.
    I'm a zombie.
    You speak. You know yourself quick what's your name.
    Name. I don't I can't . . .
    Don't think make it up.
    Ronald.

    Good what do you feel Ronald.
    Pain.
    Where it hurts.
    All over I want to go back.
    Too late schatzie too late.
    I hate your guts.

Don't be melodramatic quick describe yourself to me.
A big bag of protoplasm no shape. Very thin skin sensitive as an amoeba.
What else.
I'm a river flowing. Flowing through an ocean. The Gulf Stream.

What else.
Help me.
What else.
I'm hungry.
Ja ja mein kind I baked you a cake he goes to the stove gets one of the pies.

Ess ess he gives Ronald the pie Ronald sits up takes it hefts it in his hand slams it right in Stein's face Stein staggers back clawing whipped cream out of his eyes was ist loss was ist loss.
Ronald runs to the stove picks up a chocolate cream cake heaves another bullseye Frank stands gibbering in the

middle of the room a Boston cream pie hits him on the left cheek have you gone crazy he licks and picks at the confections lumping his face a cherry cream hits his right ear this you call gratitude he says I'll kill you screams Ronald.

Kill says Frank he spreads out his arms.

I can't I'm out of pies this is a mensch asks Frank.

There are serious things going on out there Ronald yells terrible things are happening. Is there a way to live without murdering one another. Are you trying to make a baby out of me.

First things first.

No life isn't like that. Everything at once that's what life is like. I'm horny get me a woman he screams.

Laverne yells Frank.

Never mind I'm leaving. There are serious things happening out there people are suffering.

This is news.

Our lives are an appalling slapstick. On the other side
of the TV screen real blood flows I've got to get out of this.
I'm leaving Frank slumps to the floor. Mazol he says.

Power says Ronald he walks out of the Corn Palace data
accumulates he mutters to himself. Obscurity persists
he takes out his notebook and writes it down.

Enlightenment grows he says enlightenment grows he
writes absence remains between words behind them my
pen driven by panic of empty space leaves its track he
writes it down as he says it.

Speed increases space expands my investigations proceed
but toward what is an open question everything is ambig-

uous nothing is what it is he writes it as he says it.

Evidence is ubiquitous suspicion is pervasive fantasy
hardens reality seeps away.

I have an overwhelming intuition of a plot one more
clue one more theory and everything falls into place.
Will fall.

Must fall into place. Oof.

So what are you says Tommy.

Sorry.

That's okay you just ruined my shot you realize that. I mean you oughta watch who you're bumping into when they're taking snapshots of the Corn Palace.

I was thinking about something.

You guys look I'll tell you what snap me standing in the entrance there here's the camera it's all set Ronald focuses Tommy in the viewer hey have I ever seen you before says Ronald.

Not unless you hang around La Fange, Minnesota that's

where I'm from name's Tommy. Want to snap that picture Ronald I'm a tourist what are you.

How do you know my name is Ronald.

You look like a Ronald come on I'll give you a ride you need to talk to someone.

How do you know.

I can tell by the way you keep moving your lips here's my car they get in what's the notebook for says Tommy he starts the car.

I take notes on what I say.

Why.

It's interesting I'm getting messages ten nine eight seven

six five four three two one zero testing testing abcdefghijk lmnopqrstuvwxyz ga ga ga goo goo gug gek I've said this before can't stop talking we've lost it I've been hit lost and not going to get it back let's start from there I forgot what I was going to say I forget I forgot I forget I forget thank god at last what now sodium pentathol in the beginning

darkness sound of worms crawling through vaseline thung-CHUNG e-e-e-e-e-E-E-E H-A-A-a-a-a-a-h thung-CHUNG e-e-e-e-E-E-E H-A-A-a-a-a-a-h a roaring wind followed by a roaring wind pump a rising wind and then a falling wind pump the worms the pump the wind worms pump wind repeat repeat here we are in the middle of our book speeding along on the breaking crest of the present toward god knows what destination after the first word everything follows anything follows nothing follows the world is pure invention from one minute to the next who said that.

Shakespeare says Tommy he turns into the feeder road and accelerates forty fifty sixty seventy high beams drill

into dark on U.S. 90 somebody give you a shot of speed he says Ronald sits with his hand over his mouth his cheeks puff collapse air farts through fingers mumble mumble mutter waw waw fup says Ronald can't stop it's not me get a gun who said that someone's talking in my head remember everyone has assumed an alias including you including

me zero in on reality the plot the code the infrastructure they're poisoning the air and stealing the oxygen that's part of it also selective famine *the roads clogged with completely dispossessed people who have nowhere to go and nothing to do but starve to death* they're already in partial control of your body there are ways of getting it back follow my instructions.

Hold it I need a new cartridge Tommy takes a cartridge out of the dashboard tape recorder replaces it with another hurry up this is the last cartridge he says the speedometer jumps from seventy-three to eighty-seven to ninety-three seven one hundred Nixon is in on it Kennedy is in on it

I'm in touch with Garrison anyone who knows about it is in on it or dead slow release of population control poisons into environment fallout shelters for the rich oxygen reservoirs underground anticontamination farming fear is a stick of dynamite when the fuse is lit history cancels out I say they are stealing the oxygen from the air and taking

control of our bodies am I crazy or you all right that's your opinion but remember the plot ends in death. Yours.

Faster I'm running out of tape says Tommy the speedometer moves from one hundred to one hundred three seven ten a siren starts in Ronald's head rises falls rises falls rises follow my instructions learn to read the true

meaning of events learn to breathe from the diaphragm
assume the lotos position get your head together sensitivity
training total encounter synthesis in carnal joy family
tribe affinity group we're into the macrobiotic diet learn-
ing karate yoga doing bioenergetic exercises boycotting
grapes it's everybody loving everybody like animals like a

herd of animals group flesh it's being the way you are it's
being bad it's acting bad it's good it's at the bottom of the
hole it's what fills empty space what you have inside you
what is it it's not a thing it's a shape a definition a name
it's the sound of god playing with his yoyo it's glycerol
trinitrate seventy-five percent porous material twenty-five

percent a detonator and slow burning fuse speedometer
at one thirteen seventeen the siren in his head rises rises
it's not in his head it's behind them ahead flares across the
highway red lights flash on and off.

Don't stop says Tommy he hits the brakes the car skids
straightens out hurry up it's almost over he says blah blah

blah says Ronald Tommy hits the brakes again blah blah again blah blah blah blah blah the car slows to a stop blah blah blah blah blah a man comes over to the car I want to see your license and registration blah blah blah blah blah he wears a long red scarf over a trench coat hairy mole on nose it's over says Tommy blah blah blah blah

blah blah blah blah blah blah blah blah blah blah blah blah blah blah blah blah blah blah blah blah blah blah blah blah blah blah blah blah blah blah blah blah blah blah blah blah blah blah blah blah blah blah blah blah blah look out he's got a gun.

5

Wake up. Everything up to here has been a movie.
What's going on where am I.
Hi. Experience is a code to be broken by the intelligence. I'm from the intelligence. Get your hands up.
Do you have to point that at me. What do you want.

Tell me your dreams. Lie back on the couch keep your hands up his head looks like a skull scalp shaved sharp nose thin lips behind thick glasses his eyes appear to bulge blue-white immobile his body is covered by a long black gown go on he says.

Black men chase me through high school corridors up
and down the cross hatched iron steps.
Go on.
They aren't enemies possibly they're friends.
Go on.

Hairy Nose shadows the White Asp dead fish eyes. A
bubble pops a cat stretches a petal falls. Your mother
thinks she's queen shit.
Go on.
When I wake up I'm on vacation but we have trouble

with the luggage in the elevator and then the cab driver
won't start. What moves you I ask he says Dinah might.
Go on.
My girl friend disappears these things happen.
Go on.

That's all Skuul nods.

The black men want to take over the high school and you're not black it's nothing personal says Skuul. Actually they are sympathetic and helpful. The two strange characters keep an eye on one another they cancel out. Later the

shadow become the shadowed naturally they use aliases. One carries a fish home for dinner probably flounder. Before dinner he visits his wife's boudoir bubble bath pet cat flowers. He's your father. Your mother is queen shit. In any case all this is a dream from which you then awake. The

trouble with the elevator and the cabbie at the beginning of vacation shows how events conspire. It indicates a plot. The job of intelligence is to uncover this plot. Maybe Dinah is your girlfriend evidentally the cabbie likes her too. Her disappearance is really nothing so unusual these things happen. Skuul nods. As you can see everything falls into place.

Thank you clarity at last.

None of your lip Sukenick.

I'm serious I don't know how to express my gratitude.

I feel you are the kind of rare person one doesn't meet with very often nowadays.

Well these are difficult times.

I love you do you mind my saying that.

No make a move and I'll plug you I'll blow your fucking

head off you'll be so much swiss cheese.

How can I love you and not move.

Don't love me says Skuul.

All right I have a confession I made in my pants. Is that moving.

It doesn't move me what did you make.

Dirties. All kinds you'd like them pear-shaped square-shaped chair-shaped bear-shaped air-shaped what moves you.

Dynamite.

Should I unzip my pants.

Don't be a baby says Skuul.

All right if you're so smart what's the answer.

The answer is honest systematic investigation. Careful sifting of data painful word by word exegesis of evidence till the theory of it all starts to crystallize that will en-

lighten us as to cause and effect account for deviation rationalize history and explain the future. Such slow protracted effort may seem dull to you but I can assure you that discipline has its deep delight. Don't move.

Of course but there are many disciplines you practice a

discipline of abstraction I practice a discipline of inclusion. You practice a discipline of reduction I of addition. You pursue essentials I ride with the random. You cultivate separation I union. You struggle toward stillness I rest in movement.

Don't move.
What divides us is a matter of temperament.
You can move a little.
And the consideration that abstraction is false reduction delusive essentials non-existent separation unnatural still-

ness inhuman.
You're too shifty. I could fix you with my gun.
But beyond that we're linked by delight. All art is based on delight yours as well as mine that's why I still love you.
Are you gay.

No just happy. I like to put things together I don't think it matters much what they are. Connection develops meaning falls away.

This is stupid I'm leaving says Skuul.

Don't go I need you.

For what.

You're my connection.

Sukenick why aren't you home writing your book.

I've got a short circuit listen to this. This morning I get up I check the ocean out for whales as usual the young

housewife next door steps into the patio wearing an unbelievably short red minidress now get this SHE BENDS OVER to pet the cat she stays that way thighs hams crack all BARE and gleaming in the sun I can't believe it I focus the binoculars it's true it's true bare blond and beautiful I have discovered the TRUTH and adjusting the binoculars make every effort to etch its lineaments on my mind forever but all such moments of enlightenment are as transitory as they are gratuitous she stands up. Now ever since then I don't want to write my book until I can find the

connection between it and the bare truth of my vision. Connect me Skuul teach me what I have to be taught.

This was no accident says Skuul. My analysis is that the young woman also loves whales she too enchanted by the lazy grace of the flukes the gala spouts the intelligence of

their bulk the pure fact of such size fed by the warmth of one heart. Every morning she gets up and scans the sea one day she notices you at your window with your binoculars immediately distinguished from all the humdrum people around her who couldn't care less about whales. For days she watches just as you watch watches with you soon watches you more than whales. While you watch only whales. So this morning she watches you and broods presses her thighs together separates them with her hand her husband is at the office watches broods at the window steps out

of her stepins and rubs. Her pussy reminds her of her pussycat she picks it out of its favorite corner in the kitchen near the stove goes into the yard drops it on the ground glances up at your window aims and bends over stays there till she feels your eyes burning into her soft hams branding

R on one S on the other bears the heat of it as long as she can then stands up and scurries back inside. Her name is Pixie. You love her. God knows what will happen tomorrow but much remains today for example when you leave here you meet Empty Fox. Now I have intelligence reports associating this young woman Pixie with Empty Fox through the type of affinity group known as a soft cell. There's your connection.

Skuul lowers his gun. Sukenick gets up and touches his shoulder your analysis is a work of art. It moves. It moves

me. It makes deep nonsense of my trivial sense.

In other words I've failed again he hands over his gun Sukenick takes it aims at Skuul's forehead says your fate is failure mine is flux the top of Skuul's head disappears in a pink splash accompanied by a loud bang.

All this happens in Chamberlain South Dakota which is on the east bank of the Missouri River the Missouri is wide enough around here let me tell you get a ride in a semi across to Reliance all high barren bluffs on the other side that's where you leave the farms behind and the prairie

starts rough rolling scrubby cattle ranges and you start
seeing them cowboy hats and there's always high mountains
somewhere over the horizon and that's where the wind
starts streaming glaciers rip out of the north slam into the
highway pushing cars over a whole lane I get a ride in a

pickup truck have to just about lie flat in the bed not to get
blown away I tell you that wind was aiming to blow South
Dakota over into Nebraska and maybe the whole damn
mess into the Gulf of Mexico we go through Kennebec
Presho Vivian Murdo in Kadoka we stop to give a ride to

this Indian he leaps in huddles down into his denim jacket
expressionless the truck cuts through the Badlands I jump
from one side to the other to see the colors incredible formations far out he sits in the bottom of the truck eyes
closed in Wall we stop for gas he opens his eyes. How-kola

get your lousy bad prahna workshoes off my forty-two
dollar Tony Lama boots he says.

Sorry I say I move my feet.

He nods.

I'm Ron Sukenick he holds out his hand we shake Empty

Fox he says the truck starts by now the sun is going down
the eastern sky is grey the moon is shining the west still full
of light sky deep blue suddenly Empty Fox gets up stares
intently over the cab of the truck into the sunset the east
gets darker there are a few stars now the western horizon

explodes behind us black for a while we speed along on the
edge between day and night the sky ahead luminous then
darkness gulps us we careen toward the receding light as
toward a final exit Empty Fox still staring into the west he
touches my arm points there he says I see a line of jagged

darkness thrusting into the sky like the mountains of doom
Black Hills says Empty Fox I go there the dark tunnel
stretches to the horizon the exit recedes shrinks disappears
it's night the wind dies ahead clusters of lights float in the
darkness.

Coming into Rapid City says Empty Fox we stop for a
hitchhiker he climbs into the truck very stiff we pull him
up a short fellow with crew cut pasty pudgy face not young
he has a small valise the truck drops the three of us on the
outskirts of Rapid City the little fellow opens his valise

starts working with some struts and colored paper very
quickly he has this box kite set up red and blue with small
wings he gets in and takes off rises to the top of a tall
cottonwood tree and gets off on a branch on one side starts
climbing disappears on a branch opposite he's going to fall

disappears his head pokes out around a distant branch he
falls reappears at the very top of the tree disappears around
to the other side a foot comes out from behind a branch a
leg an arm waving then he reappears next to us on the
ground I hug him he seems rather grumpy pulls away

closes up his bag walks down the road he's a clown he's
going to the circus a van pulls up looks like an old bakery
truck full of silly teenage girls we throw them off drive into
town we get off here I say we get off at a corner in front of
a bar the van moves on we can see through the rear win-

dow that the driver's seat is empty on the back of the van
it says *the spirit moves us* this is a dream Empty Fox's
dream or maybe my dream the truck drops us off on the
outskirts of Rapid City let's have a serious discussion says
Empty Fox. What's your ambition.

I want to write a book like a cloud that changes as it goes. I want to erase all books. My ambition is to unlearn everything I can't read or write that's a start. I want to unlearn and unlearn till I get to the place where the ocean of the unknown begins where my fathers live. Then I want

to go back and bring my people to live beside that ocean where they can be whole again as they were before the Wasichus came. That's why I like to travel this way. I have money for a car I have been in many movies you see my boots also my stetson very expensive the best. I carry

nothing with me when I need something I buy when I finish with it I throw away these lousy Wasichu things anyway my Indian things my father keeps for me. Anyway I very much love good things even when they are Wasichu things. Anyway I like to travel hitching that way I don't know the way to go I let Mr. Road take me. Maybe Mr. Road knows the way to go maybe not but I don't know it. I been all around the world that way Japan India I studied yoga but I never find the right way. Anyway I know I will find because I have the old Indian ways my father teaches

me my father is a medicine man very old he remembers Crazy Horse. Mr. Peyote helps me sometimes I take peyote since I was six my father gives it to me I can see things for example I saw you coming out of the Corn Palace in Mitchell this morning I wasn't there. Sometimes I have

visions like the vision you saw in the truck just before about the man who flew up to the tree that was my vision only I saw it through you. That vision has seven meanings only none of them are important what's important is the feeling of it you can't understand this. Anyway that was

your feeling in the vision. When I travel like this hunting
the unknown I don't think you don't hunt Mr. Fox by
thinking you become Mr. Fox. Anyway I don't think I let
things think through me that way I travel very fast you
can't understand this. Anyway if Mr. Road tells me to go

another way before then I go another way but he tells me
to go to the Black Hills again I don't know that till I'm in
the truck so I go to the Black Hills again which is the
sacred hunting ground of my people a very holy place
where once there were many wapiti. Also I recognize you

in the truck from my vision before but I don't know about
you because I don't like Wasichus very much they murder
Sitting Bull they murder Crazy Horse they murder many
many of my people women and old men and babies at
Wounded Knee they break their treaty and steal our sacred

hunting ground to make another Disneyland and litter its mountains with those big statues of your lousy bad prahna presidents they break the sacred hoop of our people and they're never satisfied you know all this. Anyway I don't know about you till I have my vision through you and I

learn something in that vision so tomorrow I rent a car and we go to the Black Hills together. Now I have to think a minute because when I have a vision I like to make a song or picture about what I want to remember in it.

We walk along on the shoulder of the road the wind

dead silence ahead the lights of jetliners landing and taking off soundless at an airport on the edge of town above many many stars more silence the quiet is like a bandage on a wound.

This is a translation in Lakota it's much better says

140

Empty Fox he recites in a slow practical chant
                    Without the wind
                    The kite is dead
                    With it everything
                    Is possible.

   That night we stay in a Y next morning Empty Fox
comes around driving a rented Cadillac we head up route
16 into the Hills around here they call them hills they get
way up over seven thousand feet even now these mountains
very strong medicine says Empty Fox there are shining

caves caves that breathe water runs uphill. A little north is
the geographical center of U. S. this is one of the magic
places where everything comes together. Around us dark
delta shaped pines cover the slopes with their geometry we
pass many motels concessions billboards that say *gravity*

mystery area see water run uphill anyway says Empty Fox
the Wasichus make Disneyland of all this so they can sell
it they get Indians to pretend they're Indians they make
believe these beautiful mountains are beautiful they pretend that magic is magic they make believe the truth is the

truth otherwise they can't believe anything. There is a
place with a billboard of a mountain in front of the mountain you Wasichus can't see without pretending to see so
anyway you don't believe it. Anyway that's why you all
have cameras you're not friends with your eyes only with

your minds you can't understand this.

The wind is up again springing out around curves
slamming across hairpin turns the Caddie shuddering over
long granite drops we stop on a shoulder amid weird
pinnacles massy involuted formations for a distant view

of the intruding presidents those are your gods you can't
see them unless they wear those masks says Empty Fox.
The old gods are still here and I can see them just by
looking he waves his arm toward a creased and involved
granite cliff across a canyon where I see mittens boxing

gloves elephants intestines vaginas then suddenly peering
and disappearing in the rockface strange ghostly faces
decayed bloated withered creased by age distorted brutish
skulls some of them whole figures hunched and twisted
sad mournful vindictive some horribly angry changing all

the time I jump back hah says Empty Fox. You see and
you're scared you're right to be scared the earth is very
angry she cries to her brothers the wind and the fire and
to her sister the ocean already the wind is rising and the
ocean sings back

Everything will wash away
It is good
A new race is coming
and the fire sings
Everything will burn to ash

It is good
A new nation is rising
and the wind sings
Everything will sweep away
It is good

A clean spirit is breathing.
They hear a thrashing in the woods wapiti says Empty Fox
an elk emerges in the underbrush on the other side of the
road antlers like bloody candelabra strips of skin hang
ragged from their branches makes a maddened plunge

toward a tree trunk impact of antlers shakes the tree he
rubs them against the trunk plunges again in places you
can see the pink-white of exposed horn shedding his velvet
a sign says Empty Fox the elk tosses its antlers and thrashes
off into the woods they drive further up into the mountains

wind still buzzing around them come to a high clear lake
reflecting rock formations like huge thumbs granite peaks
far end of the lake dammed by a procession of giant rocks
they stop at a campground beside the lake empty except
for a large camperbus at the other side Empty Fox gets out

he moves slowly across the campground first in one direction then another an abstracted look on his face eyes vacant
it's as if he's being moved around the clearing circles in on
one area moves backward sideways stops begins to stamp
the earth with his feet softly at first harder very hard as

if trying to drive his feet into the ground stands legs apart
waves here. Bring the tent I get the tent out of the trunk
we set it up driving the stakes deep against the wind unroll
sleeping bags Empty Fox looks at the sky snow he says.
How do you know.

The way things sound. The way things smell. Birds
flying low. Now you have to make friends with this place
the rock here is granite very old anyway older than Rockies
these trees all spruce. Come we go on trail we walk around
the end of the lake the wind is glacial I'm freezing now

look around on ground the ground is covered with chunks
of glittering stone pink translucent green deep red silver
mostly agate mica quartz here says Empty Fox. Many beautiful stones in these mountains also silver gold he spits. For
that the Wasichus break treaty now you take a stone.

Any stone.

No not any you take a stone that speaks to you I look around carefully what do you mean speaks to me.

When you see a woman and right away you fall in love before she looks before she says words she speaks to you.

You pick a stone that has that feeling.

I look around finally pick up a large jagged pink stone glittering many-faceted with glassy fractures orange layers deeply translucent faulted to its heart I feel an indefinable connection with it I hold it up to Empty Fox good this is

your stone it's good luck we continue along the trail along the base of hollow cliffs through passages under tall rocks that lean on one another or hang precarious odd shapes figures faces giants petrified on the brink of life Empty Fox stops in a green bowl of cliffs that dwarf the tall pines now

you go back to our place you make friends with your stone
he points at the mountains to one side I go up to Harney
Peak. This is the highest peak till you come to the Rockies
a very strong place he's wearing rings I haven't seen before
on his left hand a silver ring with an irregularly geometric

figure of a bird indented in its face on his right a heavy
turquoise ring with a turquoise bluer than I've ever seen
the same color as the deep mountain sky above us only
flecked through with veins of silver and gold I have to
make friends with the wind he says he moves on up the

trail I go back to the camp bending against the wind.
    I sit hunched in front of the tent I look at my stone
smell the pine smell listen to the wind I look at my stone
turn it over and over weigh it in my hand put my nose to
it rub it against my cheek lick it bite on it look at it some

more hold it up to the sun feel it warm in my cupped hands eyes closed run my fingers along its sharp edges try to remember its shapes map its faults it facets its idiosyncracies make it shine in the light this way and that I look up. Something is different dark green of pines more intense

blue of sky deeper granite rocks sharper denser the picture postcard lake more convincing the ground more solid I love this place I'm flooded with love for it. I lie down and put my cheek against the earth breathing deeply slowly then a strange thing happens. I feel heavier warmer my

body flows tingles quivers glows I feel the gravity that connects me with the earth passing through me like a current like a responding love the sun hugs me the sun is in love with me I get up breathe deep I can't understand this. Then the words come into my mind I don't know where they come from the secret is that there is no secret.

Seen the buffalo yet a smiling portly man in a red nylon jacket and orange earmuffs smiles into my face.

What buffalo.

You mean you haven't seen the buffalo yet we took them

down this morning they loved it they got a whole herd down there got some good shots too. Color.

I haven't seen them.

What about the cave you seen the cave yet jeez you don't want to miss the cave that's the best part we took them over

there yesterday. They went crazy.

Did they.

Oh jeez. You been to Rushmore they went wild at Rushmore. I thought they were gonna get arrested a little overexcited you know but they loved it all right.

Good.

Yeah they loved it all right they sure got a lot of stuff here don't they this is more like it. Like I was saying to my wife. We were going to spend it all in Yellowstone but they were going crazy. Geysers you know. Big deal. You

seen one geyser know what I mean I mean all right water squirting out of the ground but they got entirely too many geysers there if you ask me. This is more like it. We went over to the Tetons. More mountains. Big deal that wasn't more like it but this is what I call more like it boy that

was the smartest thing I ever did in my life coming over here. Smartest thing I ever did in my life. Especially what with the camper you can't beat this place for camping boy that camper. That was the smartest thing I ever did in my life too come on over I'll show you around we go over to

his camper it's gigantic about the size of a Greyhound bus.
Smartest thing I ever did he says this is my wife Veronica.
My name's Henry Aldrich. Hi there.

I'm Nick it's all going away. Unreal. We board the
Queen Mary that's what we call her hah-hah-hah this is

the rumpus room picture windows on both sides leather
armchair card table foldup ping pong table this is where
we store the bicycles here's the bar that's the galley the
bridge is up ahead captain's quarters two TVs one here
one in the crew's quarters aft are you a veteran.

No.

I thought you might be a veteran I was a Seabee jeez
those were the days weren't they scotch.

No thanks he pours himself a scotch Henry you had
enough today says Veronica ah come on willya a rifle pokes

its way out of the crew's quarters a real rifle bah bah bah bah I gotcha I gotcha lousy gook.

Ah there they are says Henry I tollya not to play with the rifle it might be loaded.

A fat kid and a skinny kid run into the rumpus room

the fat kid has the rifle the skinny kid has a helmet and bazooka not real we just killed a thousand gooks says the fat kid.

Nice Buster why don't you go back and kill some nice Indians look out they're coming over the rise.

We killed all the Injuns we're gonna kill him.

Put that rifle down damn it.

Hands up all of you says Buster.

Listen you fat little bastard I had enough out of you today.

He's not fat he's glandular says Veronica.
I'll murder him.
Henry.
I'm just saying that's all.
Look out it's loaded says the skinny kid Buster pulls the

trigger. Click nothing happens Henry grabs the gun slams the kid in the stomach with his fist. With his fist. Buster caroms off the foldup ping pong table onto the floor Henry gets down straddles him smacks his face smacks again from the other side with the back of his hand again again. Fat.

Little. Damn. Bastard. Veronica screaming pulls him off. Buster staggers sobbing back to the crew's quarters.
How do you like the Black Hills I say.
It's very nice says Veronica. It's something a little different.

They love it says Henry panting. It's something just a little bit different.

Well excuse me I have to go now don't you want to watch the game says Henry I stagger down the gangplank back to the tent sit down pick up my stone hold it tight in

both hands look around gone. It's all gone. Everything unreal I feel like cardboard. I'm cold this place is dull nothing to do. I'm terribly bored when is Empty Fox getting back what a drag. A movie Indian are you kidding what kind of bullshit I'm freezing my ass off what am I

doing here. This is awful. I'm lonely I need a drink. I'm just about to go watch the game when Empty Fox appears on a rock nearby. How-kola Ron he sweeps his arm toward the horizon the sun is going he says. I look around at the long rock shadows the sky is a darker blue the sun on the peaks softer more orange Empty Fox drops an armload of firewood something is missing. The wind I realize the wind has been still a long time without my noticing the air quiet chill lying over the lake like a second more transparent lake everything looks three dimensional again.

How was Harney Peak. Empty Fox laughs.
Good he says.
What did you do.
I was on the wing.
What.

Dreaming that's what I call on the wing I go very fast. I had a great dream very strong.
What about.
I make up a song. Goes like this
        It doesn't matter

Where you start
It all comes together
It all falls apart.
Empty Fox I have something to say don't take it wrong
I love you he grabs my shoulder and shakes me.

Hah. You're alive now anyway. Good. The only good
Wasichu is a live Wasichu he laughs we make fire. We
make a fire. The sun goes down I take out my candy bar.
Empty Fox would you like to smoke with me.
Sure what we smoke a candy bar hah hah hah.

This is where I keep my dope in here.
Better stay away from police who like candy what dope.
Hash.
Hash good we smoke. I get it ready he takes out a small
pipe of blood red clay.

Use my pipe he says. It's special.

We pass the pipe back and forth after a while Empty
Fox says now you are my friend Ron you are connected to
me I am connected to you both of us connected to this
place he smokes a while more the rest is postcards he says.

Soon I'm on the wing I'm in the ocean sky sunny whales
are spouting their heads break water they slide slowly to
the surface spout their long backs glide roll under with a
slow sweep of the flukes one especially surfacing next to
me a great dappled grey whale very old his immense back

mossy and barnacled I can see the bristly folds of his blow
hole a naval that connects him with his mother the air his
flukes as he sounds waving high over me like a gesture
goodbye follow me I'm choking Empty Fox has his hand
on the back of my neck holding me down on the ground

what are you doing I throw him off sit up.

You're on the wing he says he dives at me I roll to the side get up he catches me with a punch on the shoulder cut it out I don't want to hurt you I know karate I say.

What kup.

Green belt.

Too bad I'm a brown belt UTZ he lets go with a left side kick I step back catch him on the achilles tendon with a lower block that sends him spinning completely around he comes out of it in a fast pivot with a right mace hand

that just misses my temple he dodges a right round house kick to his mid-section he comes in with a left knife hand that I catch with a double arm block he trips me as I go into a front kick I stumble he drives in with an upper target punch I barely deflect with an elbow block a head

kick that comes out of nowhere grazes my ear my attempt
to counter stopped by a fancy backward side kick I manage
to back away gasping for breath he's not even breathing
hard I know one blow is enough to finish either of us he
comes in very loose hard to see his movements in the

firelight he feints a side kick comes in with a spear hand
attack to my midsection just short feints a left knife hand
UTZ catches me with an elbow to the ribs that almost
knocks me down but I come back with a reverse punch
YATZ that catches him on the chest we both get off side kicks

UTZ UTZ collide stumble back we circle one another me
gasping limping from the collision my ribs hurt I know I
can't last long I charge screaming feint a kick throw an
upper target punch he bangs aside with a left arm block a
left middle target he catches with a knife hand block that

almost breaks my wrist and lands a reverse punch to my eye UTZ just as I bring my knee up into his groin I lose my balance go sprawling onto the ground he doubles over staggers away I can't get up next thing I know he's on the back of my neck again holding me down you're on the

wing he says. He tightens his hands shakes me by the neck till my teeth chatter if you fly too far you can't come back he says he shakes me talk shakes me again talk talk canke ot'ungyakel akiuzapi no mini oihpeyapi.

Good go on what else.

Yunkan miniwanca kin ihecegla ablak hingle jonas mini oihpeyapi kin icunhan wakantanka hogan tanka wan el eca yeya canke jonas niyakel napca canke nige kin mahel anpetu yamni na hanhepi yamni t'e sni un na okiwanjila wakantanka cekiyahe next thing he knows his face is wet it's morning everything is white he's in a sleeping bag covered with snow. Alone. He feels a lump in his side he unzips the bag it's his stone he gets up his neck is sore his ribs ache thigh stiff wrist purple eye swollen it feels good his body feels serious full of its own intelligence his head

is peculiarly empty light he takes out his notebook. He writes

everything looks more real

"　　"　　feels　　"　　"

I　　"　　"　　"

then he throws away his notebook. Walks out to the road starts hitching into Custer he gets a ride right away in Custer he puts his hand in his pocket finds Empty Fox has left him his rings he puts them on he still wears them today.

4

Hi. Everything up to here has been a novel. My feeling about it so far is it's serious. But it's going to get even more serious that's also my feeling about myself. What a coincidence. Anyway that's my feeling about it on this page in any

case it's my attempt to sort out my feelings about certain things that have been happening to me lately like Pixie for example I can't get her off my mind. Is she really in a soft cell with Empty Fox I should have asked him. Also what's the meaning of the 7-3-10 numerological scheme that runs through the book and of the code message near the beginning what about the plot is it all part of a plot. If I knew that I'd probably know what's going to happen next

which I don't either in my novel or in my life. Except sometimes maybe like Ali Buba's warning about head wounds I wrote that six months before the garage door came down on my head while I was sitting in a California

patio over the sea writing this book. But this is a subject I don't like thinking about too eerie. All I know is I'm getting messages I don't know where they come from or who else gets them it's a mystery to me I just pass it on

and hope it comes together this is a message. Part of the
message is get a road map all these places are real even the
more unlikely ones I've traveled among them slept in their
campsites their motels form is when you look back and see

your footprints in the sand. Meaning disintegrates connection proliferates what does that mean. Red Desert for
example that's where Roland Sycamore is staying now
Roland Sycamore you don't know this yet peeled off from

the Sukenick character after the karate fight and the latter
is no longer a character at all but the real me if that's
possible I'm getting out of this novel. When you fly too
far you don't come back. Red Desert is in South Central

Wyoming just a fraction of a mile to the north of the Continental Divide. To the north of the Continental Divide that's right because Red Desert is at the inner edge of a huge absence in the middle of the country surrounded

by peaks eight to ten thousand feet high which drains neither east nor west but into itself known as the Great Divide Basin and do you know what's inside this prodigy absolutely nothing desert except for a drainhole in the

middle emptying into the void. So here we are at the source. Omphalos. Roland alone with his body in his room at The New Vacancy Motel thinking about the dream he just had the dream is about Pixie he doesn't know that yet.

166

The dream is about getting mugged the message says.
The dream is about getting mugged I write.
On the Lower East Side late at night it says.
On the Lower East Side late at night I write.

Somebody comes up behind Roland and puts a knife to
his throat maybe it's Jojo.
Somebody comes up behind Roland and puts a knife to
his throat I think it is Jojo.

Hand over your wallet or you're dead says Jojo this is on
a dark sidestreet hand over your wallet or you're dead says
Jojo this is on a dark sidestreet about two AM noone
around Roland tries an elbow in Jojo's ribs the blade edge

saws across his adam's apple okay okay anything says
Roland I should kill you for that says Jojo no wallet in
pocket says Roland he can feel blood running down the
front of his neck get it out quick and don't do nothing

sudden Roland fishes out his wallet remembers a story
about a girl held up at gunpoint handing over her money
then getting shot anyway Jojo grabs the wallet at that
moment Roland smashes his fist up against the wrist of

Jojo's knife hand whirls slams Jojo's temple with his elbow
kicks him in the balls picks up the wallet and knife helps
Jojo to his feet for some dreadful reason Roland has to
help Jojo to the Avenue he puts Jojo's arm around his neck

168

half drags half walks him down the street Jojo all the
while muttering I'm gonna getchew man gonna cutchew
up gimme back my knife you cocksuckuh gonna get my
friends gimme it now maybe I letchew alone gonna kill

you cocksuckuh maybe this week maybe next week I
getchew you fuckin cocksuckuh when they reach the
Avenue Jojo won't let Roland go Roland heads for his
building you gonna take me up to your place you motha-

fuck I'm gonna kill you cocksuckinmothafuckuh two men
are talking in the vestibule Roland knows one of them help
he won't let go says Roland use that knife says the man it
says. Use that knife says the man. This dream completely

changes Roland's life.

This dream completely changes Roland's life.

It has seven meanings it says it has seven meanings three are important of those two are that knife=wife that's why

it's about Pixie secret bride of the White Asp the other isn't about Pixie the one that changes Roland's life isn't any of them it's the one about the can factory the feeling of the dream is like the can factory Roland thinks to him-

self it says. It shows how I can. The can factory. The can factory is in Brooklyn on the waterfront it makes tin cans Roland needs a job. Badly he looks for three weeks finally at the can company he lies he begs he flatters he promises he lies he lies he lies his way into a job he's a tire. A tire stands at the end of one of the production lines and ties. He ties the cans as they come off the line in stacks of ten with wire knotted tightly so it cuts into the flesh of your

fingers Roland rubs the growths on his fingers middle and index of each hand and that was twenty years ago. Roland starts slow he can't keep up with the line the cans pile up then he can keep up then the line can't keep up with him

in a week he's the fastest tire on the floor fastest tire ever the other guys start coming over at coffee break the crooked shop steward hints at letting him in on the bonus from the crooked speedup system there's even talk of the foreman making him a flanger if there's an opening. A flanger flanges the bottoms onto the bodies of the cans the bottoms are thin coated steel disks with sharp serrated edges that often fly off the crooked unsafe flanging machines whirling

at enormous speeds slicing through whatever flesh happens to get in their way most often the fingers of the flangers on the other hand they get paid a lot and it's more prestige. There are very few people on the floor with ten fin-

gers the person with the fewest has five between both hands he can't flange anymore. But as long as you have six fingers you can always make a quick buck flanging and everybody on the floor was always trying to get enough together for some personal project quitting taking a trip to Vegas moving to a trailer colony in Daytona Beach opening a bar but they always blew it. So one day at coffee break the foreman pats Roland on the shoulder you got a

future here kid keep it up and next time one of the guys gets a finger sliced off who knows meantime whirling can lids are flying all over the place and Roland starts getting a little bored with the five quick motions needed to tie a

bunch of cans repeated say sixty times a minute one day he bends down a whirling can lid whizzes over where his head just was that's exciting at least. One day one of the guys comes over she's a woman in fact but she's thought

of as one of the guys named Rosie Rosie shows him her tits
it's her way of being flirtatious to be precise she doesn't
show all of them but only three or four she has eight or
ten in rows from ribs to armpits he's never counted the

guys on the line used to kid her show us your tits Rosie
and she would say how many and show them she was a
good sport well that was fun too but it got on Roland's
nerves. Meantime Roland is getting extremely bored with

tying and he doesn't think he wants to get into flanging
but he can't quit because he won't get unemployment. So
then Roland's efficiency graph starts going down even
faster than it went up he can't keep up any more the cans

pile up on his table the pile gets higher it gets up over his
head then it topples over cans rolling all around the floor
Roland chasing them people tripping cursing the crooked
bonus for the crooked speedup shrinks to almost nothing

on line number three the crooked shop steward hints about
putting some muscle on Roland but he's beyond that
cackling as the cans tumble around him he gets fired
laughing while the man who hired him looks hurt I give

you a chance we never have to fire a tire before. So that
teaches Roland something he doesn't know what but something. Now he knows that's the first time he tuned in now
he's tuning in again he can feel it happening he feels

empty. And expectant 987654321. 0. Omphalos. Roland
casts the I Ching it says.

Roland takes out his copy of The Book of Changes.
What should I do now he asks he casts the coins. Roland

casts the hexagram Shih Ho Biting Through. He turns to
Biting Through a thunderstorm is coming it says. Look
out for a traitor and tale bearer. It's dangerous to stay still
to avoid permanent injury move at once decisive action is

needed. Force is necessary but avoid violence stop evading
your responsibilities you may get off easy this time but
only if you mend your ways. Be aware of the dog. Your
way requires clarity and excitement.

Shih Ho changes to P'i Standstill Roland looks up Standstill. You are living in a period of decay learn to deal with confusion and disorder it says. The best lack all conviction and the worst are full of passionate intensity.

Though outwardly hard weak and inferior men are in control. Don't work on what's been spoiled nor be drawn into public life this will only expose you to danger. A withdrawal to inner understanding is required before you

will be able to bite through. You will succeed and make money if you avoid success and financial gain. Be frugal. You may be forced into exile for a time. Movement bites through stagnation and disunity. A streaming together.

A knock on the door who is it says Roland the door opens.

That's okay I use my key I'm the proprietor of the establishment a heavy balding man fat fingers glittering

with massive rings so. What are you.

Get out.

Your name is he takes out a pad thumbs through Roland Sycamore. Right.

Get out. Who are you.

Name's Tommy I turn up. You want your message or not.

What message.

From Toro from our friends you want it or not.
Are you a member of our friends.
Would I know about it if I wasn't a member you want it
or not.

From Toro.
Yeah.
Toro's dead.
It's his dying message.

What is it Tommy pulls out a scrap of paper it says
            sale
            not
            seize

what's that supposed to mean says Roland.

You're supposed to know now you have to give me an answer we're having a meet Roland turns the scrap of paper over writes hands it back to Tommy.

i l it says. What's that supposed to mean.

Figure it out says Roland he pulls his knife it has a matchstick under the blade for fast opening Roland holds the blade arm extended six inches from Tommy's heart

don't make me kill you he says I'd like to so much don't make me.

Okay says Tommy he backs out the door cracks his knuckles be seeing you he says he leaves that's not Tommy

the Tourist thinks Roland to himself that's Ruby Ger-
anium he's from another story I can tell by the way he
cracks his knuckles Roland walks out of his room crosses
the road takes his chances with the night. He heads away

from the Red Desert Country just outside of town he
crosses the Continental Divide now he's in the West. The
moon is full he can see he's moving into hilly rangeland
grass sage chaparral his forty-two dollar Tony Lama cow-

boy boots feel right at home somewhere just over the
horizon high mountains this is fun. He walks for hours
plays tag with tumbleweed watches falling stars high on the
smell of sage plenty of moonlight no fatigue. The moon

goes down before dawn he takes shelter next to a rock as
he nods asleep he hears cattle lowing in the distance he
awakes in the early sun stiff cold surrounded by beautiful
grazing horned animals tan whiterumped white chestpat-

terns darker head markings when he gets up they freeze
for an instant run off with amazing speed disappearing up
a hill like antelope in a cave painting. He walks south-
southeast according to his map there should be a dirt road

somewhere in that direction he walks for many hours this
time he's tired he's hot he's thirsty he's lost he hears the
sound of the Brooklyn Dodgers playing in Ebbets Field
before a sellout crowd a hallucination of course it goes

away it comes back this time it sounds like Dixie Walker
is up with the bases loaded 1942 some kind of audial mirage
it goes away as he climbs the crest of a hill it gradually
comes back fades comes back the Pacific Ocean he hasn't

walked that far at the crest of the hill he looks down into
a huge crowd gathering encampment what way way down
in a natural bowl in the hills tents campfires thousands of
parked cars it disappears as he descends into a gully reap-

pears as he crosses a last crest the smell of grass coming up
from the bowl is enough to turn him on as he comes down
into the fringes of the crowd people turn and stare mostly
kids children adolescents in fantastic gypsy costume many

nude to the waist including girls he sees a girl nudge a
boy and point as he goes by is it him someone asks the
crowd noise seems to develop gratuitous crescendos then
subsides a section starts clapping and shouting for no par-

ticular reason nothing is happening is it him someone asks
again say what are you all doing here Roland asks a boy.
We're not sure yet we're waiting says the boy. Someone's
put acid in the drinking water far out says another kids

are freaking out all over the place screaming tearing their
clothes off being sick tackling one another a nude adolescent wanders by holding his erection hey you're neat he
screams I dig it he leaps on a teenage girl pawing at her

184

clothes wow fuckinfarout says another girls watching this
is loony Roland thinks to himself hey is that him says a
kid the crowd seems to make way for Roland as he walks
toward the center he's looking for the men's room maybe

something to eat seems to be some kind of comfort station
in the middle of the crowd a tent long banners huge colorful intergalactic flags hey it's him someone says someone
repeats word runs through the crowd it's him it's him

silence strikes the festbowl as he reaches the comfort station
where's the men's room he asks a tall bearded Viking the
Viking waves toward the hills at the edges of the crowd
this is the freakout tent he says is that you.

No says Roland.

You better tell them he hands Roland a mike it's not me Roland's voice booms through the bowl I mean I'm not him. He hears a gigantic clattering above a helicopter

appears low over the hills stops hovers about a hundred feet above the crowd this is an order to disperse it says its voice is metallic this is an order to disperse anyone who does not immediately disperse will be considered subject

to arrest. There are gunshots a line of mounted cowboys charges over the crest of a hill firing their guns into the air yip yip yip the kids watch them galloping down the hill cheers and applause come up from the crowd they think

they're watching a western the cowboys barrel down the
hill beating the flanks of their horses they think they're in
a western they hit the edge of the crowd whipping people
with their ropes left and right plunge in full speed with

their horses the kids over there are getting trampled stam-
peded the crowd starts milling they're trapped in the canyon Roland thinks to himself the only chance is to get
them over behind the cars so they can walk or even drive

out of the bowl otherwise Roland speaks into the mike
everybody start moving toward the parking lot don't panic
don't run get over behind the cars so you can walk or even
drive out of the bowl nothing happens. Nobody listens the

crowd starts churning in on itself people running from the horses trample on people ahead of them the cowboys shooting lower over the heads of the crowd shout as if they're herding cattle girls are screaming Roland's voice

booms out through the festbowl listen I'm him I'm him the people around him stop and turn do you hear me booms Roland it's me I'm him. People stop and look his way it's him it's him who is he. This is me talking says

Roland listen to me listen to me don't panic everybody start walking toward the parking lot do not run everybody get behind the cars it's your only chance everybody move toward the parking lot the direction of the crowd starts to

shift a drift starts toward the cars a flow Roland hears
motors starting up cars are pulling out the cowboys still
working their way through the crowd whipping trampling
yip-yipping tents sag and go down horses ride right through

them get that guy something grabs Roland around the
chest and arms pulls him over he's bouncing along the
ground the rope slips almost catches around his neck
doesn't Roland blacks out somebody gives him a hand pulls

him up he's shoved along by the crowd now and then
everybody starts running Roland runs with them in the
parking lot it begins to thin out they reach the dirt road
there are more cowboys charging at them up the road the

crowd wavers flows back into itself hits the pressure coming from behind rushes forward like surf spewing rocks bottles sound of shots a boy next to Roland falls the back of his head missing it's spattered on the face of the girl behind

him Roland is being shoved off the road uphill sound of shots a flash an explosion no thunder again rolling through the canyon the sky is black clouds burst it comes down in huge drops Roland still running already soaked the ground

turning into slippery mud as he gets over the top of the hill people are falling getting up falling again as they race downhill sheets of rain turn the hillside into sheets of shoe-sucking mud people scatter slow to a walk drift into small

190

groups plod through the rain the rain stops groups and stragglers are walking over the hills in every direction I have to rest says a boy in Roland's group. Keep going we better put some distance between ourselves and those guns

says Roland. They trudge over sludgy hills after a while the sun comes out after a while a girl comes up to Roland we're tired how about resting for a while. The other groups have disappeared nothing but rangeland quiet. Guess it

looks okay now over there says Roland they flop down near a rock on the crest of a hill Roland can see twenty or thirty miles either way nothing.

What do we do now a boy says.

Why ask me says Roland he feels grouchy he's getting a
cold sore throat constipated can't think. The boy shrugs
my name's Lowell he says good says Roland.

My name's Jack says another.

Good says Roland.
Mine's Bruce.
Good.
I'm Emoretta.

Good.
I'm Jim.
Good Jim.
My name's Avron.

Avron.
I'm Karen.
Karen good.
Richard.

Good.
Anne.
Anne very nice.
David.

Good.
Sherry.
Good they all have names they all give him their names
after a while he loses track stops listening just keeps nod-

ding good good. I'm hungry says one after they finish giving their names. Hungry I'm thirsty says another me too says Richard me too says Lowell or somebody else Bruce starts passing around a joint. Or somebody else. Jack

is holding hands with Sherry Emoretta starts making out with Jim or somebody somebody says I think we're lost somebody says yeah complaints we getter get moving says Roland.

Are we lost.
No says Roland.
Then what's lost something's lost I have that feeling.
We're here. It's lost.

Which way should we walk.

This way follow me Roland has no idea which way but wants to avoid complaints they walk for quite a while we're tired someone says.

Keep walking.

We need water.

Keep walking pretty soon they hit a trail worn into the hills they follow it for a while far out someone says they all

stop. The trail leads into a draw at the bottom there's a pipe sticking up with a drinking fountain on top of it they go down and drink.

How'd you find it says Richard or someone.

Luck says Roland.
Are you a finder.
Get off my back.
After resting they continue on the trail after a while a

Dalmatian trots up to them Roland likes Dalmatians he
makes friends with it the Dalmatian wants them to go off
in another direction at an angle from the path he dances
off that way back to Roland off again calling in his doggy

barreltone what's up Spots what's over there Spots barks
greying pink muzzled looking wise Roland cuts off the
trail follows Spots Spots pokes his nose into Roland's palm
leads them into a gully there's a shelter set up inside boxes

of canned goods fruit juices crackers everything Roland
opens some dog food for Spots they eat rest after a while
Spots starts barking he wants them to come down the gully
load up says Roland they take supplies Roland walks after

the dog the gully opens out onto high tableland high
mountains on three horizons Spots is sniffing at something
up ahead of them funny webby footprints embedded in
the rock very big these are dinosaur tracks says Roland

Spots is already up ahead wagging barking sniffing at another set they follow the dog from one set of tracks to
another this goes on for a few miles Roland looks behind
him he has the vague impression that there are fewer in

the group hey where are David and Sherry here and here
they say they continue down the dinosaur trail next time
he looks around there seem to be even fewer where's Jim
Jack and Emoretta here here and here they say they con-

tinue in the track of the dinosaur after a while Roland
whirls Anne and Richard he yells no answer where's Anne
and Richard everybody looks around and shrugs Jim Jack
and whoever no answer David and whoever no answer

there are very few of them left in fact five or six maybe
more like four or five they look around in a bewildered
way sort of sheepish at having lost so many of themselves
without noticing but still eager for whatever comes next.

198

Here the dinosaur trail branches into alternatives Spots touches Roland's hand with his nose awaits directions one trail leads down into a broad arid valley another up into a high isolated butte. Which way should we go they ask.

I can't tell you which way to go.
I thought you were a finder.
Listen stop bothering me. You been following me around now for a whole day it makes me nervous. Don't

crowd me leave me alone. I don't know anything more than you do.
Why you holding out on us.
Come on why don't you beat it says Roland.

Which way you going.
Up there he points to the butte.
Man you kidding we're not going up there. You crazy.
Why you going up there.

More interesting. Looks like you can see for a hundred
miles from up there.
You'll never get anywhere that way they say Roland
leaves them standing on a set of dinosaur tracks and fol-

lows Spots up the trail when he gets to the top it's near
sundown but it looks like he can see for a hundred miles
mountains on four horizons some with snow he can see the
path he just climbed the places where he almost fell he can

see the whole valley the other trail led into he can't see the rest of the group anywhere. No trace of them. Anywhere. He feels lonely. Spots he calls. Spots. Spots he yells. Spah-ots. He whistles here boy Spah-ots. Nothing. A little

wind sweeping across the top of the butte. Over below the far side of the butte he spots a highway with an easy path leading down to it. He heads that way gets a ride into Dinosaur another through Utah with a man who tells him

that one pair of houseflies if their offspring survived could within six months cover the earth forty-seven feet deep with houseflies he gets off in Panguitch. Checks in at a place on the edge of town The Oshose Inn—A New

Vacancy Motel takes his key starts for his room wait a minute who's he.

He just checked in Mr. Derrekker Mr. Derrekker is a tall smooth man in leather pants and leather shirt this

motel is for my people get him out.

Yes Mr. Derrekker.

I don't suppose you found the watch yet. No that would be too much to expect. That watch is very precious to me

I can't work without that watch. It's my lucky watch. We've already lost two days damn it do something.

We've looked everywhere Mr. Derrekker we're still looking.

Your watch is in the fishbowl in the lobby says Roland.
What do you know about it get him out of here says
Derrekker.

Roland shrugs starts to leave wait a minute says Derrek-

ker. Is there a fishbowl in the lobby.

Yes Mr. Derrekker.

Go look the clerk comes back with Derrekker's dripping
watch Derrekker glares suspiciously at Roland how did you

find it.

I'm a finder Roland starts to leave wait a minute says
Derrekker. Let me think. Derrekker closes his eyes presses
his fist against his brow stays that way for thirty seconds.

Ah he looks up smiles. I can use you. We don't have a
finder. We need one. That's just what we need. A finder.
Are you from Huge.
I don't follow.

This is a Howard Huge production. We're on location.
We're shooting a movie called "Panguitch."
Is that why you're on location in Panguitch.
No that's just an accident. It's an epic-mythic-cosmic

spectacular about two aboriginal South American gods
named Popocatepetl and Titicaca. Popocatepetl is a leg-
ended revolutionary in modern Mexico talked of by the
peons as a reincarnation of the old god in such cases you

get the Precolumbian elements side by side with a kind
of peasant populism the archaic god informed by popular
culture an attempt to sustain the primitive against the
trauma of the present or maybe the present against the

trauma of the primitive cargo cults for instance I don't
understand any of this. But that doesn't matter. What
matters is the visual image the old peon as the movie
opens telling a story about Popocatepetl as he tells it cut

to Popocatepetl actually living through the story get it we
see him in a room with his girl the police break in the girl
is immediately raped and shot Popo is thrown naked into
a prison cell fade to bull ring Popo still naked is pushed

into the arena they release a black fighting bull Popo face
in hands sinks to his haunches crying and shaking drooling
a sound starts in his belly his face turns up to the sky an
ow-ow-ow a howling louder and louder longer and longer

the bull stops shuffles around the howl changes to a roar
shaking with rage Popo charges mace hand to nostrils knife
hand chop snaps off a horn double two finger gouge to
eyes knife hand snaps other horn round house kick to head

Popo finishes him with a spear hand to the neck cut back
to old peon. This is the story they tell. And then in his
sadness Popocatepetl was heard to say out of defeat comes
triumph. Out of defeat comes triumph. Out of defeat

comes nada. Palabra palabra. Men are beasts. Cut back to arena they give him both ears the tail the horns four hooves the cock and finally the whole bull. And he says give cock and bull to the poor. As always. How's that for an

opener. Dynamite.

What happens next.

Next Popo gets a message from his wife Titicaca it goes like this

$$1\,1\,1\,1\,1\,1\,1\,1\,1\,1 = I$$
$$o\,o\,o\,o\,o\,o\,o\,o\,o\,o = O$$

From this Popo knows Titicaca has been gangbanged. By ten men. That she liked it. That she comes from Iowa.

That she's turning into a cow. That she wants more. That that's a lot of bull. That she's full of shit. That she owes him a fuck. That he's won. That he's won nothing. How many times can one go into nothing. Do you follow.

Perfectly.

Well maybe you can explain it to me. In the next scene a bovine Iowan gazes out the window of a tourist cafe below the snowy cone of a Mexican volcano pan to vol-

cano. Cut back to cafe where the woman from Iowa orders a bottle of pop and reads about the Pope. Outside the caca-birds are calling *shittit shittit shittit*. The woman is reflec-tive passive placid as a lake. I know this day is a special unfolding inevitable and full of secret meaning one senses the completion of an eschatology a solar countdown the horizon shapes the final zero draws tight tight says Orlando sitting next to her. O she says she speaks with a heavy

Spanish accent from a hanging plant a cat leaps to the floor a petal falls a deep rumbling shakes the air. She runs into the street arms outstretched. Orlando is furious. He screams kicks spits shits. Many years later he meets a

buxom waitress named Titi. Cut to many years later. I won says Orlando. O naughts answers Titi she speaks with a heavy Spanish accent. Cockatu responds Orlando the exchange seems to be in some kind of code. This takes place in Panguitch Utah. And that's where we are now if you think you can cope with all that you're hired. I need a finder. I need someone who can find out what the hell is going on in this movie. I mean I like it as a work of art

of course but it needs a lot of revision if it's going to get any box.

Sorry Mr. Derrekker I don't make revisions says Roland.

That's DerREKKer. Look this is a Huge Production.

It's big. Very big. It's got everything. Panguitch is in it. You're in it. I'm in it. We're being filmed right now the cameras are rolling all the time we have them set up all over the world what chaos. Look please help me I don't

know what to do next I don't understand all this. I don't
know what Huge is up to this time I think he's in over his
head if you ask me.

Didn't he ever give you a hint.

Well I only saw him once to tell you the truth. When
he hired me. I did most of the talking I was giving him my
conception of his conception the trouble was I didn't know
anything at all about his conception. He just stood there

playing with his yoyo the man is a wizard Derrekker flushes
with admiration. I've never seen anybody do things like
that with a yoyo. A wizard. Beyond belief.

What did he look like.

I can't remember he was big maybe he had a beard. I remember how he would nod every now and then and say seven and three is ten and you know I've thought about it. He was right. Only I still don't know what the hell he was

talking about. I think he's Jewish.

How come.

Because of this telegram he sent the Greek director Kakaboulie who was Director of this property before I

was hired it says Yo. all hands get your shit together you're id Rx i.d. soft tit camera action why oh why oh I o i oi.

What else.

The only other thing I have is a crank letter from the

weekly paper written by a local bullshit artist under a pseudonym. Some say it's by Kakaboulie himself it says Dear Huge received yours of Sunday it's all Greek to us polloi here but we try to dope it out I just pass it on I do

my best man of multimillion masks my admiral I ask for wisdom you give me shit what kind of crap is that I try and tune in but all I get is static crack snaggle plop very cacaphonic do I wrong you or write you who am I signed

Anonymous Bosh. I sympathize with that how do you like the script.

Hard words nice music.

You like it.

I think this movie is what's happening.
You do.
I think Panguitch is where it's at.
Then you take the job.

No.
If it's money there's a lot of money in this. Name a price the sky's the limit. I'll give you carte blanche I want a creative film something original something a little

different who's your agent. Work up a treatment take your time submit it in two weeks you can use your own ideas anything you want.

You're too late I don't have any ideas. About anything.

Anymore. He walks out of the room out of the motel past the bellowing guard dogs out of the dream onto the highway walks south no moon no carlights no starlight stumbling along the shoulder lonesome as the last goodbye

nothing noone nowhere ouch who's that.
 Ouch who's that.
 Roland.
 Arnold.

Arnold which Arnold.
 From New York.
 From New York do you know a guy named Carl.
 Carl from the Bang Gang.

Yeah Bang Gang Carl.

Sure I know all them guys.

No kidding you know Carl how do you like that what a coincidence my god I can't believe it. How is Carl.

He's dead.

Carl dead.

Had an accident with a stick of dynamite. They identified him by his bridgework.

Oh. How about Scott.

Scott was shot. In a police station. Resisting arrest.

How about Ova.

Hanged herself in a jail cell.

Rex.
Disappeared in a swamp near Memphis.
Nixie.
She went mad.

Velma.
She's a junkie.
Harrold.
Brain damaged from a beating. He's a vegetable.

Nick.
Serving one to ninety-nine.
What about Nadia.
Killed by a rapist.

What about Alma.
She married an executive.
Alma too how about Trixie.
Turned state's evidence.

Donald.
He's got cancer.
Any other news.
Not that I can think of.

Well gee it's been awful nice bumping into you Arnold
I was feeling kind of lonely.

Me too you can call me Arnie let's hitch up okay the only
ride they can get is into Bryce Canyon National Park next

morning they take a trail into the canyon past Thor's
Hammer The Cathedral The Wall of Windows The Two
Sisters The Seven Dwarfs The Angels' Landing The Twins
The Devil's Outhouse The Three Sisters Satan's Belly-

button Old Nick's Torture Garden Hell's House of Hor-
rors Lucifer's Leap the signs say it is dangerous and un-
lawful to go off the trail they go off the trail on a shortcut
through The Devil's Sphincter get stuck on a steep gravelly

ledge too loose and steep to climb back up sliding slowly
on the treacherous incline toward a high overhang above
a jagged dropping gulch Roland heads for a rocky prom-
ontory finding foothold on a tiny ledge that crumbles

under his foot as he leaps catches a jutting rock pulls himself up climbs down to the gulch. Arnie is sliding slowly toward the overhang it must be a fifty foot drop he sits down lies down spreads his limbs he can't stop himself

jump says Roland comes to the edge in a sitting position draws his feet back from the emptiness jump says Roland I'm going to die he thinks to himself broken legs seem like unbelievable good luck his feet are sliding over his ass

jump yells Roland at the last second he pushes off aiming for a clear spot gives in to the fall lands on his feet with a numb shock rolls down the gulch bouncing off boulders hits Roland's shoulder knocks him over both sprawl roll

bounce slide to a stop my ankle says Arnie.
 That's all.
 Yeah.
 That's nothing.

It hurts how do I get out of here they look around at the
steep sliding treacherous debris of the canyon wait a minute says Roland. He unlaces Arnie's boot around the
swelling works it off his foot Arnie squirming and sweating

rolls down the sock feels the ankle could be broken wait
a minute. Roland squats takes the ankle in both hands and
concentrates what are you doing for christ sake taking a
shit says Arnie.

Shut up feel any better says Roland.

No Roland works into the ankle with his fingers squeez-
ing massaging relax he says breathe deep in out in out he
holds the ankle between his hands feel any better.

No. Yes. Hey it feels better what are you doing to me.
Breathe Roland concentrates he can feel the swelling
subside the skin goes from purple to lavender to black
and blue to green to normal it feels much better says Arnie.

Get up and try it Arnie tries it it feels all better what
are you kidding me what's going on shut up says Roland
they climb out of the gulch walk out of the Canyon catch
a ride into Vegas Roland goes into a store buys Arnie a

stetson gee thanks how come says Arnie they go into a casino Roland looks around at the slot machines picks one puts a dollar in hold your hat under there he says he pulls the handle the dollars pour into the hat holy shit

says Arnie. A thin old lady with impossible red hair limps over sputtering that's my machine I just went for change her face is purple.

Give her the money says Roland.

Are you kidding.

Give it to her Arnie dumps the dollars on the floor Roland picks another machine hold the hat under it he says he pulls the handle the dollars pour into the hat holy

shit says Arnie do it again Roland does it twice more
dodges through the crowd around them walks to a car
rental garage they head out Route 16 through Arden Jean
into California both of them high on their own momentum

the speed of the car through open space catching up
caught up arrival we're here it's here this is where it's at
Roland turns on the radio flash an A-bomb blast at the
testing grounds has leaked an atom cloud into the atmos-

phere Vegas on evacuation alert oil spills on the coast
earthquakes reported near Los Angeles avalanches in the
Sierra Nevada flooding mudslides in the hills in the south
brush fires burn out of control the seals facing extinction

from DDT pelicans seabirds whales dying out fish poisoned
bodies of young girls washed up on beaches cult murder
victim gutted eaten mass murder victims found in home
bombing arson rape suicides double for fifteen year olds

and people in their twenties something is moving much
faster than we are Roland and Arnie think to themselves
something we'll never catch up with so that when we
finally get there it's always somewhere else or maybe it's

something that's catching up with us.

Well if you can't catch up catch on says Roland the
smog starts out in the deserts blankets the orange groves
thickens over the cities hides the mountains above Santa

Anita they get there just in time for the daily double what are you going out to says Arnie the track he has it all figured out the favorite in the first race You Haul is a sure thing forget it and Ear Muff looks good in the second

at five to one they put down ten dollars each on the double You Haul finishes out of the money and Ear Muff runs twelfth oh well you can't win them all says Arnie yes you can says Roland.

In the third race Arnie likes Escalation at three to one or Crazy Wasp a long shot who comes from behind. Escalation has finished second in his last two races fading in the last furlong but at a longer one and a sixteenth and the jockey's hot Crazy Wasp has only had two races both out of the money but looks good in recent workouts Arnie bets Escalation and Roland Crazy Wasp Crazy Wasp finishes fast but out of the money Escalation fades in the

stretch and comes in second. They drop fifty dollars on You Stink in the fourth I guess he's only good on turf says Arnie.

We have to split up says Roland. Don't cry Arnie starts

crying.

What am I going to do now says Arnie. Roland gives him the money keeps two dollars picks a horse in the fifth without thinking about it Out to Lunch Out to Lunch comes in at eight to one.

He puts sixteen dollars on Yoyo in the sixth still not thinking Yoyo comes in at five to two.

He puts all his money on I Owe You in the seventh

for no reason and hits eleven to two.

His mind a blank he picks On the Wing in the eighth who comes in at thirty to one.

Concentrating very hard on nothing he picks Yoo Hoo

and O Zone one and two in the ninth race Exacta and wins so much money they have to give him a certified check after he fills out the special income tax forms. He feels a little sick he wonders what to do next he goes

through his pockets pulls out an old shopping list it says
> sea salt
> Iodine
> manhattan clam chowder.

Reading down Roland immediately understands he's to
have his eyes examined. Reading across suggests he find
an eye doctor close to the ocean he heads for Santa Monica
sees the Pacific for the first time it's very different from the

Atlantic he doesn't expect that Roland makes a wish he
wishes he were bigger stronger calmer then he finds an
optometrist I. Askew he goes in the doctor is a thin sun-
tanned old fellow leathery neck eyes that seem to focus

around rather than on Roland's face the words come into
Roland's mind he sees into the invisible where do they
come from you have an aura says I. Askew.
 Of what.

Of nothing first a few questions what sign are you.
Capricorn.
You're lying.
Of course but I don't call it lying.

What do you call it.
Getting it together.
Good do you feel you have a secret.
Yes.

What is it.
I don't know.
Good did you ever have a very high fever as a child.
Yes.

Delirious.
Yes.
Hallucinations.
Yes.

Have you ever seen flying saucers astral bodies anything
like that.
Yes.
Ever seen anyone with a halo anything of that sort.

Yes.

Very interesting now cover your right eye and read this chart top line.

s s

Middle **line.**

a i l

Bottom line.

n   a   z   i   s

Good now cover the left eye top line.

s   a   l   e

Middle.

n o t

232

Bottom.
s e i z e
Good now cover both eyes top.
s a i l

Middle
k n o t
Bottom
s e a s

Very good extraordinary he feels around Roland's brow
sits down behind his desk stares intensely at an area above
and possibly just behind Roland's head taps his desk taps
his desk taps his desk this is my diagnosis you're developing

what is sometimes called second sight don't get nervous.
It happens much more often than you might think usually
to people rich in experience who are approaching some
kind of maturity as with the poltergeist phenomenon and

adolescence it is associated with a certain time of life but
usually is censored by the mind even as it is perceived
since most people lack the capacity indeed the inclination
to contain such powers let alone use them. One sometimes

hears of this experience in such terms as the third eye
clairvoyance etcetera I prefer to avoid the spectacular it
simply means that you can see more than other people.
Actually it might most simply be put under the category

of heightened sensation in general for some indeed it comes through hearing as in the third ear experience others generate enormously heightened tactile perception and develop a facility with the socalled laying on of hands

procedure others a sense of smell keen enough to substitute for sight even taste I've even heard of one man whose palate grew so refined he could taste the quality of another's thought. Actually the extension of any of the senses

is usually accompanied by a heightening of all the others to some degree so that if you are to become let's say a seeing eye man for the rest of us you might expect to have certain other talents in tow also. However a warning. You are entering a transitional phase the metaphor is teething. Or better replacing your baby teeth or better getting your wisdom teeth you'll have to put up with a lot of pain oh you'll have your satisfactions too more and more but I

mean you may not want or be able to tolerate it I don't know your capacities it's up to you. Actually one hears about more and more of these cases almost in such numbers as to make one conjecture about large scale chromo-

some changes and viable mutations time will tell. I'm going to put you in touch with the Los Angeles area group it will probably help they meet down along the coast south of here he takes out a prescription pad what did you say your name is.

   R.

   How do you spell that.

   A r r.

   First initial.

   R.

   Good here you are Mr. Arr Askew tears off the sheet gives it to R it says I. Askew Optometrist Rx R. Arr 73710

   S. Coast Blvd. 10 PM Sundays admits one that's in Laguna Beach let's synchronize watches says Askew.

   What are we in four.

   Right we have four minutes leeway going on three 987654321

3

zero he gets back in his car drives south on the freeway he
hits severe wind conditions coming down from the mountains a hot dry wind that slams into the car carrying sand

and grit drives heavy clouds of dust toward the ocean he's
terribly thirsty enormous balls of tumbleweed go bouncing
across the highway. Santanna says a gas station attendant

238

bad for the fires the roads are blocked south and east when
he hits the coast he sees a blackish-reddish cloud moving
over the hills hanging out over the ocean snowing grey

ashes the heat is exhausting he stops at a motel in Balboa
with the sign of a nesting eagle it has a patio overlooking
the ocean he wants a place where he can hear the waves

breaking the motel is called The Balboa Egress—Another
New Vacancy Motel.

Pixie's apartment is on the second floor across the patio

at right angles their bedrooms have a common wall. The
name on the mailbox is W. A. Sprakk W. A. Sprakk is
also known as W. A. Spat alias W. A. Spawn alias W. A.

Sprat alias Whitney Asparagus alias W. H. Aspic alias
W. Asperin her husband is a well built blond lout heavy
suntan he leaves at eight A.M. sometimes with suitcase

sometimes stays away several days seems to be part of his
job. The way they fuck is she never wants it tells him he's
a bore that's all he wants from her he doesn't love her why

doesn't he jerk off with his surfboard he's just a stupid jock
he has no refinement get away from me dammit you're not
getting anything off me no no not again oh shit oh god oh

my god give it to me I love you that's her thing. His thing
is come on cunt cut the crap lie down I'm horny he only
grunts once when he comes like a man driving home a

spike otherwise it's all Pixie moaning grunting yelling R
can hear it all through the cinderblock as he masturbates
their beds must be right next to one another on either side

of the wall before long R is in love he always falls in love
in bed he digs watching her sunbathe in the patio especially when she turns over and unties her bikini top so he

can see the sides of her tits once or twice even a blond
nipple sometimes he gets her in his binoculars while he's
scanning the ocean for whales what he likes about her is

she's so refined she gives piano lessons in the afternoon.

There's a bowl of fresh sage on the table I. Askew
introduces him R. Arr Iz Iz is a sharp dresser snappy as a

242

hound's tooth glad tameechiz says Iz he has one of those
old time Brooklyn accents R feels close to Iz right away
R feels Iz has something to teach him. Sailor is next Sailor

looks a little like Popeye bulging biceps knobby elbows
pipe tatoos grizzly hair he knots unknots a length of rope
R. Arr Sailor yo says Sailor. Next comes colorful Remark-

able Ramona a good looking lady still young seductive
voluptuous dressed like a piece of meat mini motley deep
dish decolleté hi there says Remarkable Ramona. Felix

Feelie is a foxy man foolproof animal eyes funny fleshy
face it's not funny he feels R's cheeks with the tips of his
fingers you have problems like everybody says Felix Feelie

shake he gives R the thumbshake R goes around exchang-
ing thumbshakes with everyone sits down next to Iz. R is
an eye says I. Askew I ask you as an eye how is he coming

through.

Felix Feelie runs his hand down R's back across his
chest his belly he's like a knot somebody untie him says

Felix Feelie.

Sailor lifts his nose sniffs like a dog in R's direction he don't smell right to me Sailor knots unknots his rope.

Whakina bullshitchew kiddin me says Iz. Not a knot just not. Not yet. He got no taste fuh chrise sake who's kiddin who. I bin true dis trip catch da Sea Beach Express

at Turdy-Fort. Strictly BMT. Baby Misses Tit. Bowel Movement Training. Bar Mitzvah Tomorrow. Bite My Tochus. Dint I know you in 2B. P.S. 101.

No.

Well 2B or not 2B it's da same ting. Yuh still aint says Iz.

I'm getting news from the Interior sh-h-h says Remark-

able Ramona. Relinquish imperishable imponderables. U.R. Ur. What goes in must come out. Wake up to the present the promised land.

What's that mean.

Don't know wait there's more. February 9. Go to the beach. 10. That's all.

I really dig you says R.

Of course he digs her he's from the east. He's got an interiority complex says Felix Feelie.

Sailor puts a kindly hand on R's arm get lost he says sincerely.

Hot day. Beaches filled with bearded boys their dogs

girls in teasing bikinis proud of tits bulging around tiny loose tops nipples pushing through openknit bottoms below crack of ass sunripe cheeks. Happy flesh. Death is not inherent in life but in specialization thinks R. Animals not complexly specialized have a greater capacity for regeneration. There's so much exposed flesh on the beach it

reveals itself to R as a generality something deep in his gut responds to this generality he smiles at some of it it's blond it smiles back.

Nice day says R far out she says she could be anywhere between sixteen and thirty R sits down she's sitting up on her towel her top two loose triangles that play hide and seek

with her tits a wave crashes been swimimng says **R.**
Before is it cold you get used to it.

See any whales says R not swimming saw some from the

beach today they're really neat she leans on her elbow a
nipple pops out she pushes it back unruly thing smiles a
wave crashes shaking the beach R points to her Mr. Nat-

ural comics reading.

In this sun wow I can't even think they watch the surfers
for a while a half hour passes the sea crashes gee this is fun

isn't it she says.

Yes it is says R after a while after a while he says that's a nice bathing suit she smiles he takes her hand they lay

back he can hear her breathing deepen she releases his hand I think I'll turn over she turns over would you untie my string he unties it she works her top out from under her

hands it to him could you put that over there now both of them are breathing deeply a half hour passes the sea crashes wow this is fun isn't it she says.

Let's go for a walk says R okay could you hand me my top please.

For a kiss says R she smiles okay she says she pushes her

breasts against his chest they kiss keep kissing they stop you're a really neat dude she says. They get up for a walk where we going she says I don't know says R they walk

through the town in bare feet and bathing suits end up at R's car he drives into one of the canyons above the town then off on a smaller road that leads into the rangeland in

the hills and ends they get out where we going she says
don't know says R they stumble into a grass lined gully
she takes off her top lies back around them meadowlarks

chuck doubletongue and gurgle there's a rank almost shitty
smell this is real trippy she says R is uptight he grabs her
hand look I'm not exactly an ascetic but you're getting a

little ahead of me what's ascetic mean she says R doesn't
answer.

Don't you think I'm sexy she says you're so sexy it's not

even sexy says R I mean we haven't even talked.

Don't talk do she says he embraces her do R thinks to himself do that's too simple he takes her bottoms off I

can't make this he says.

Why not she says it's too easy I'm not used to things being so easy he kicks his bathing suit off starts doing rubs

his penis against her wet crack fondles her nipples she climbs on top comes down after a while he stops doing his body starts doing things he didn't know it could do he's sitting up she on his lap facing him he feels like he's way up into her womb he feels it clutching and unclutching as she starts to come he leans back onto a soft mound just in

the right place he pumps up and down using it for leverage he feels unbelievably huge it's coming he holds it back it's coming he holds it back coming he holds he can't hold

it comes it comes in such a long uninterrupted spurt he wonders where it comes from his whole body is in it all his feeling is in it his mind drains down into it then it

comes again and then again and then again when he's
finished it comes out of nowhere one more time his mind
goes with it for a minute he almost stops thinking com-

pletely maybe completely what bliss all he knows is her
womb still clutched tight around his cock and then it
comes again. He stretches back arms over head his belly

starts shaking a spasm rises into his chest his gullet another
out his mouth it's a laugh he starts laughing he laughs and
laughs then she catches it she starts hugs him both of them

rolling on the ground laughing he rolls off the mound beneath him it's a pile of horseshit it's all over his back it stinks he points to it it's good luck he says they laugh even

harder he flops on it rolls in it on his belly they laugh so hard they can't stand it tears are coming out their eyes soon they start crying what are you crying about he says.

　　　　　　　　　　　*

Don't know what are you she sobs don't know how you feeling.

Good full you she says good happy empty they drive

back can't talk sorry he says you don't have to why not.
Too empty he says he drops her at her car I think I'm
getting simpler I think a lot of us are getting simpler on-

togeny reproduces phylogeny is the reverse true R thinks
to himself what's your name he asks today Trixie tomorrow
Pixie she says she drives away.

R wakes up Pixie is doing her thing but she's alone
W. A. Sprakk left with his suitcase R can hear the bed
springs creaking Pixie moaning again again love me don't

love me don't love me don't love me after a while a groan
it stops R is in love he can't stand it he writes her a note
it goes U.O.I. seen the white ass i.d. familiar if so I demand

bare truth here's a wet crack why is the fox devoid because
he fox himself empty let me fill you in M. T. Focks he
sneaks it into her mailbox. So next day he walks by her

chaise in the patio was that Chopin you were playing
yesterday says R.

Why yes.

I like the way you play.
Thank you.
Do you think you'd like to play with me sometime.

Do you play an instrument.
No.
Then I don't understand.

From the first time I saw you I knew I'd like you.
That's very sweet.
Is your husband away.

Yes he is.
You must be a little lonely.
A little.

Perhaps you could use a little company this evening.
That's possible what's your name.
M. T. Focks.

I don't care if he shits you call this a soft sell. Are
you the one who sent this weird mash note she pulls out
a crumpled piece of paper. What language you speak

anyhow eskimo you must be some kinda nut.

I love you.

Love my ass you send me another one a these I'm gonna

call the fuckin cops I mean you got a nerve on you she balls up the note throws it at him goes in starts playing loud patriotic numbers on her piano.

R goes to his room. Riots in the cities. There's been a violent escalation of the peace effort. The police are shooting Chicanos in Los Angeles. The borders are closed to anyone under thirty or "colored" a new official classification. Oil. Last major Pacific Coast nesting colony of the great blue heron. Seal rookeries thousands of volunteers

struggled. Pick up birds and clean their feathers. "Maybe three per cent. All this may be completely helpless." WHALES STILL MAKE GOOD PET FOOD. More

than 600,000 harpooned and cut up. Blue whale largest creature ever probably over the brink. MOBY DICK WAS A SPERM—IS FACING EXTINCTION. "But I can't really tell you why the ordinary man is so fascinated by these animals" he said recently. A glimpse of a hump the sight of a spout maybe a look at the flukes smashing down.

I can't explain the universal interest or empathy or whatever it is. From Jonah to Moby Dick. You should hear how quiet they get sort of awed. Some blues can be seen

offshore.

R watches the sunset. In front of his view of the sunset is a billboard of the sunset. Imminence of horror absence of joy. Strange huge footprints have been discovered in the northwest. R has the itch to travel again he feels slightly insecure about being in California as if the whole

thing is liable to break off and sink at any time. He listens to the silence of the ocean the near silence of the ocean. The ocean seems to speak but not quite like music its

voice rises toward speech then descends

2

toward silence always moving moving R no explanations. The alarm rings R wakes up something is going to

happen. It's February 8. Sailor comes over what's up says R Sailor shrugs. You feel it too Sailor nods what are we in two. Check two minutes leeway we better hurry Sailor says they go for a walk along the piers is it the eclipse.

Maybe Sailor says what are we going to do says R. Sailor sits down takes out his rope makes a knot hands it to R

untie it he says R can't. Keep trying R keeps trying a knot is a connection Sailor says. Sometimes it's the wrong con-

nection then you have to know how to untie it untie it R
can't. Once you untie it you have to tie it so you make

the right connection. The way you tie it is first you have
to know the right connection then you have to know the

knot for it then you have to make it with the right feeling
but first you have to untie it he takes the rope unties it

with a quick pull. There are over three thousand knots not
only knots hitches splices lashing whipping other kinds.

There's the granny the reef the square the sheet the eye
the jury the turtle the tarbuck the prusik there's mousing

marling netting belaying parbuckling there's the turk's
head the lark's head the monkey's fist the catspaw the

268

sheepshank the blood bight the carrick bend the magnus
hitch the scout's woggle the bos'n's plait the double clove

hitch the turn turl the studding sail halyard the half
hitch killick hitch those are just a few. The interesting

thing about knots is they hold things together so when
they're holding right they're not there's just the thing.

When they're keeping things apart instead of holding them together they're not really knots they're snarls that's why

people snarl and get angry when they're not holding together this is the philosophy of the knot. Or maybe of

the not since a good knot is not do you follow. Perfectly says R. Good because I'm going to teach you all about

knots not today tomorrow that's my boat over there it's
all ready to go what am I thinking Sailor says.

The blue whale says R.
Go on.

The biggest body.
Go on.

A hundred fifty suns.
No.

Tons a hundred speak tweet feet long the tongue.
Go on.

Is nine thousand pounds. Nine thousand.
Right go on.

The heart twelve hundred twenty foot lout. Spout.
Go on I'm still sending.

Beak jaw fish spine human ribs it's lonely. What's lonely.
They sighted one way out there are so few they can't

mate. They never meet says Sailor.
You want to make friends with it says R.

Check.
I can't I have things to do says R.

So what.
I have a career I want to be useful do good things.

So what.
I'm in love.

So what.
I have to get it together.

So what.
What will I learn.

The sowhatness of things.
R wakes up someone is dragging a huge safe over a

granite washboard the bed is pitching like a boat everything is rattling in the dark helpless in the grip of some-

thing final this can't go on this can't go on this can't go on
it goes on it stops it's a dream. R wakes up the sun is out

something is different it's happened. There's been a huge
earthquake houses collapsed freeways torn up hospitals

destroyed a dam is breaking power gone thousands dead injured fleeing in confusion nobody knows how many ani-

mals stampede panicky dogs roam the streets a strange line of bubbles foams up off the coast massive disorientation

sets in communications with the interior are cut off people wander around lose sense of direction sequence identity

the astronauts back from their moonwalk float out of con-
tact in midspace avoiding tonight's total eclipse of the

moon this morning's convulsion of the earth it's 10 o'clock
R has a premonition about Pixie he runs down to the

beach in time to see her washed ashore she's not breathing
he turns her on her back opens her jaw wide pulls her

tongue out of her throat with his finger pushes her head
back holds her nostrils closed gives her the kiss of life

watches her chest rise and fall again rise fall again after a
while it starts to rise and fall by itself she gags gasps starts

breathing opens her eyes closes opens it's you she says.
What happened says R I went swimming. I can't swim

says Pixie. What do you mean R concentrates reads her mind he gets nothing no input no output something miss-

ing here R thinks to himself he concentrates harder it's nothing like Sailor's fluid flow his total response his almost

zero gap between what comes in and what goes out like an animal like a superconscious animal it's a blank wall R

concentrates harder he goes into a trance he allows his
preconscious psyche to flow into her mind to lap against

the wall to flow beyond her mind suddenly he recoils a
look of pain crosses his face then of disgust then of anger

he puts her back on the sand walks off the beach when he
looks over his shoulder she's tottering back into the surf

that night the moon is full and bright then it turns pink
then red-brown then dark brown in the shadow of the

earth it's February 9 there's one minute leeway the moon
goes down like a burning ship.

1

Wake up stop this is it drop everything stop all this is a

message you've been reading now throw it away stop the

wind is blowing the tide is flowing stop finish up and get

out stop this is this this is this stop that's that Sailor hoists

the sail where we going thinks R no knowing thinks

284

Sailor I'm frightened thinks R have faith thinks Sailor

have you done this before thinks R I do it all the time we

all do it all the time thinks Sailor are you frightened

thinks R no thinks Sailor what's going to happen thinks

R ontday onay thinks Sailor otway oodshay eyeay ooday

thinks R ooklay earhay eelfay ellsmay aystay thinks Sailor

the wind fills the sail the boat moves out with the tide sun

low over mountains of Catalina in western sky a brilliant

white line appears fuzzing at edges rocket trail freak cloud jetritus blown by upper wind takes on curves and loops

of an illegible calligraphy sun going down over Catalina

blue gold orange sky scribble changing in wind letters

form AURLZY then OSSRY then QSORRZY sun down

band of gold band of orange Q S ORR Y sky darkens in

east cloud doodle takes shape of hand a hand offered or

waving or pointing Q in palm the word SORRY emerges

turns many colors in the sun fading from upper sky

striations of blue red violet orange SORRY blows away

hand flushes with color dissolves takes on contour of blue

whale stars out in east whale luminous becomes boat hull

becomes pointer pointing seaward this way out becomes

question mark becomes ghostly white seabird wings sweep-

ing sky endures to night stars boat rocks like a cradle way

out R's emptiness floods with flow of S's mind sky dark sea

wash salt smell wave spray ebbs into vacancy around him

the cradle rocks this way this way he's coming close an

alarm rings not an alarm a sound a shadow of a sound i

approaches o io is yo no more leeway 987654321 wake up

this way this way this way this way this way this way this

way out this

way out

O